BOSTON JONSON IN
MURDER BY BURGER

I0551878

Biff Mitchell

BOSTON JONSON IN MURDER BY BURGER

DOUBLE DRAGON

Introduction

What takes place in this novel in the future is true. What takes place in the present is lies-as the future will tell.

"No great product was ever greater than its marketing."

- Gansheng Barto

Chapter 1 - Eat It

It was the kind of place of which question marks are made. The ceiling disappeared into shadows high above several hundred square feet of buffed oak floor that formed a giant circular checkerboard. A leather chair in the center of the room faced a wall of tall windows with thick fog curling outside the panes. Each of the other walls had dark wooden doors framed by stone arches with vague coats of arms in their centers. Dozens of eight-pronged chandeliers dropped from the ceiling and hung a dozen feet from the floor like big bronze spiders with electric butts. Fifteen feet above the floor, and surrounding the entire inside of the room, a balcony that appeared to be carved from a solid chunk of mahogany posed its own little mystery. There were no stairs to the balcony, and no doors.

It was one hell of an ornament.

White marble statues of what looked like ancient Greek and Roman gods were pushed up against the walls. Most were naked. Some wore robes. They all smiled and winked. A four-legged creature with bat-like wings and an ugly half-dog-half-pig face bit into a marble cigar.

A man lay on the floor, his back propped against the wall. Beside him a marble breasted woman winked at nothing and nobody in particular. Around the man the air trembled with the smell of fear and food. His eyes protruded under horn-rimmed glasses as he watched his hand slide across his bare belly where his shirt was torn open. Bits of foodstuff spattered his navy blue dress jacket. More of the stuff, mixed with saliva, splotched his white beard. His face glistened with sweat as his hand moved slowly across his chest. He whimpered as it pushed what looked like the most perfect hamburger in the world against his lips. His jaw shook and his mouth quivered and his face twisted, but his lips parted and his hand pushed the burger in. He chewed and he swallowed, chewed and swallowed and whimpered and chewed some more until his hand was empty.

Then his hand fell to his side and grabbed another cold but perfect burger from the packing box and slid it over his stomach. As he watched the hand, a scream pushed through the masticated burger oozing down his throat and broke from his lips like a muffled belch. Blood spurted from his bloated stomach, sprinkling red spots on his hand, marring the golden perfection of the burger bun. Blood poured over his stomach and into the fabric of his white shirt. Blood gurgled out as the rip in his stomach lengthened painfully, and still his hand moved toward his mouth with the bloody burger.

***

Somewhere else, someone was thinking: *A promise is a promise*.

8

Chapter 2 - The Spit

Tangerine hair flowed over Boston Jonson's shoulders. He couldn't remember it being less than shoulder length and it never grew longer, as though each hair reached his shoulder and said, "Time to stop." and stopped growing. It was something he tried not to think about. He paid the driver and the MagCab floated noiselessly away on a layer of furious electron activity between the magnetic bottom of the cab and the strip of metal buried under the road. He turned and faced the building.

It was a giant twisted thing in stone, rising out of the never-ending fog in what used to be the downtown harbor area. Blue, yellow and red flood lamps spotlighted flying buttresses, abutments, gabled doors and pyramid-shaped pinnacles in the sprawling mist.

Barto Burger headquarters soared seven hundred feet into the fog and occupied all of what used to be the downtown core of Saint John, one of North America's oldest cities. The Barto Burger building was the largest Gothic cathedral in the world. In fact, it was bigger than the real ones, the ones with priests and nuns and God, and what better place for it than a city shrouded in unrelenting fog for three decades, a wet little footnote to the global warming story. Because of the fog no one had ever seen the entire building, but what could be seen was impressive with its intricate mazes of buttresses and ornate towers and thousands of gargoyles with a steady stream of condensed fog dripping from their fanged mouths.

In fact, it was the dripping mouths that inspired the locals to name it The Spit Church, and later just The Spit. Dozens of those locals stood solemnly in front the main entrance about fifty feet away from Boston holding signs with scrawled messages:

DIE AND GO TO HELL, BARTO!

GET OUT BARTO BURGER! GET OUT!

EAT-COLI!

They spit right back at the gargoyles.

They were the Spitters, and they'd been spitting and protesting for over two decades. They'd protested the demolition of historic buildings in the downtown core when the building was no more than a rough sketch. They'd protested all through the zoning laws, permits procedures, surveying, environmental impact studies, demolition phases, digging and landfill phases, and the actual construction. They'd been there every day, every night, week-after-week, year-after-year, taking turns, enlisting their children from tyke to teen to adult, keeping the signs waving, the spit spewing, and the hatred growing.

Fortunately, Boston didn't have to wade through that dew-crazed crowd. He looked up at the Gothic building. His eyes were slanted, almost sad-like, or maybe querying, or perhaps tired. There was something of temples and old men in orange robes in his aqua eyes. Or maybe a favorite blues tune. His mouth was square, strong, like his jaw. He wore black pants and a blatantly unapologetic Hawaiian shirt.

He walked like memory passing through time, like his body slid around molecules in the air so as not to disturb anything but people in his passing.

He stopped. He looked up. He looked down. He closed his eyes. He breathed deeply and slowly. He tuned his ears to his surroundings. He relaxed his shoulders and neck. He breathed slower, deeply, rhythmically, like a slow-moving pendulum. He soothed his mind to sleep and nudged his soul awake and allowed himself to become a conduit into sheer left-brain knowingness. Boston had a theory about vibrations. They were everywhere and they were everything. They were pure energy and they were timeless. They were the stuff of events and the fairy-dust memories of all that had passed. Boston knew instinctively that all he had to do was stand perfectly still and listen with the ears of his soul and he would feel the sound and texture of those vibrations. They would tell him what had passed. They would recreate events and make known that which was mystery. He stood. He listened. He breathed.

And, as always, nothing happened.

He walked across misty pavement to an ornate stone arch framing a small wooden door that looked like historical flotsam from something squeezed out of the grandeur of Louis XIV's court. As he looked for a knob or a handle or a buzzer, the door opened.

In keeping with the décor, it creaked.

A tall man in a dark brown robe with matching hood stared at Boston. A mouth, supposedly attached to a face somewhere in the shadows of the hood, said, "Mr. Jonson. They're expecting you."

Of course they were. They'd asked for him to be assigned to this.

Boston stepped into a stone corridor that smelled of ancient times. The builders had even grooved the stone floor and smoothed it over to give the impression of thousands of travelers' feet wearing it down through eons of use-in just under twenty years. Small electric lamps in the ceiling spread light grudgingly through the narrow space.

The robed man lifted his arm like a cotton wing and pointed toward an open elevator door. Its warm fluorescent light appeared otherworldly, as though it might be a magical time machine. Boston walked into the light and the doors slid quietly shut, locking him inside.

Somewhere in this gargantuan throwback to feudal times, a man was dead, and Boston Jonson, tangerine hair, Hawaiian shirt and all, was needed.

Chapter 3 - Boston Jonson, CI

In a world ruled by crime and crazy people, police forces around the world fought an uphill battle with barely enough cops to go around and not nearly enough funds to compete with the bad guys. Police recruitment was a joke. Nobody wanted to be a cop in a world where crime and craziness were easier to get into and the payoff was a hell of a lot more attractive. Law and order were losing ground in a desperate swim up the pipes of a toilet that never stopped flushing.

In response to the crisis, a retired cop named William Bailey determined that the single biggest problem facing police forces was having their time wasted on things that weren't really crime-related, things like suicide and domestic disputes that didn't involve one human being bashing the brains out of another human being. What was needed, said Bailey "was a filter to screen out the crap from the crime."

That filter was Consultative and Referral-based Investigative Criminal Channeling, or CRICC.

CRICC treated crime like a disease, and it trained people to take its pulse and decide what to do. Its "doctors" were called Consultative Investigators, or CIs. When a suspected crime was reported, a CI was sent to the scene to assess the situation and make a recommendation like a doctor's prescription or referral. The recommendation could range from "no further action required" to "refer to following agency, organization, specialist" which could include police departments, private investigators, criminologists, holistic investigators, social workers, shamans, the media, next of kin, or any one of, or combination of, several thousand other possibilities, including "other." The recommendation could also state, "further assessment required." But this was rare.

Boston Jonson was the Cream de Menthe of the CI crop. His specialty was events involving human death. The event involving human death that he was on his way to assess at the moment would prove to be different from anything he'd assessed before, though he had no idea how he knew this. Perhaps the vibes?

Chapter 4 - A Giant Hollow
Caramel Square with Chandeliers

There was only one way to describe it: a giant hollow caramel square pulled by giant hands to make the inside form a long golden hall with chandeliers and teak panels with shiny brass lamps. Boston stepped from the elevator into a hall of such mellow luxury you could almost eat it.

Another robed figure pointed, this time toward the far end of the hall. Boston nodded to the faceless hood and plied into a river of carpet. He detected a hint of cherries and mint in the air. In spite of the line of crystal chandeliers and brass lamps, the light was soft. The air was warm and womb-like.

Boston breathed as he walked, breathed deep with his eyes narrowed just enough to keep himself on course but still block out most of the visual stimuli. He relaxed, breathing deeper and slower, feeling the pendulum of his soul slicing through the passage of time. He opened himself to the hall. He became the hall. He welcomed the vibrations of the hall into his body and mind. He willed himself to yield to the vibrations, to feel the vibrations, to learn from the vibrations and to become one with the meaning and reality of the vibrations.

He tripped and nearly tore a brass lamp out of the wall to stop diving face-first into the carpet. He looked back, smiling shyly, but the hooded man was gone. At the end of the hall he walked through a somber mahogany doorway and into what looked like a huge round checkerboard with a leather chair in the center. Another hooded man pointed toward a far wall where a man lay on the floor, propped against the wall, mash dripping from his mouth, eyes wide and dead. A white cardboard box lay open beside him, and all around him the floor was littered with paper wrappings. Figures in dark brown robes fussed around the body. Boston said, "Don't touch anything."

The figures stopped. Hoods turned toward Boston and then toward a man in a white robe standing a dozen feet away from the body. His hood was down around his shoulders, revealing a massive red-cheeked head. He nodded and the robed figures backed away from the body. Boston walked up to him and extended his hand, "Mr. Beaton?"

"Yes, I am Mr. Beaton." He spoke slowly, as though he were checking each word for accuracy and correctness. Boston had to crane his head up. Beaton was easily six and a half feet tall, and big-not fat-big. His short dark hair looked like something pasted to the top of his head. Even his small face looked pasted onto the front of his head as an afterthought. His mouth was open and quivering like something grafted from a fish. He stared right into Boston's eyes. Not looked, stared. Boston met his eyes dead on.

"Hello, Mr. Beaton. Boston Jonson, CI."

"Yes, of course. We sent for you." He pointed toward the body on the floor, still staring at Boston, and said. "We expect this will be handled with the utmost discretion, Mr. Jonson. The gentleman on the floor is Gansheng Barto. Himself."

Gansheng Barto! thought Boston. *This limp messy thing on the floor is the great Gansheng Barto. Himself.*

Chapter 5 - Get Wealthy In Just Five Years

Gansheng Barto, President, CEO and co-founder of Barto Burger International, had granted just one interview ever. It broke every download record at NewsFromAllAroundTheWorld.com. Breaking with the ezine's usual interactive, hypertext, exploratory, non-linear, media-rich, bandwidth-hungry format, there had been just a few screens of text and a single picture showing Gansheng Barto as a young man at an unidentified wedding. His red curly hair blended into his red beard giving his face a pronounced roundness. What was most compelling about the picture, though, were his eyes and his posture. It was hard to tell the color of his eyes behind the glasses but their cold stare into whatever lay beyond the borders of the picture was chilling. His posture was relaxed, confident and deadly, like a panther eyeing lunch. A white carnation and white shirt cut a clear contrast with the deep blue of his suit and tie.

The interview was short on details of his early years-not surprising considering that around the age of twenty-five he'd been found wandering the streets of Shanghai, naked except for a wrist bracelet with the word "Barto" inscribed on it.

Barto: I remembered nothing of my past. My name, who I was, where I'd come from...it was all blank.

Interviewer: And then a Chinese family...

Barto: I have no family.

In one of the hundreds of stories spawned by the interview, Boston had read that a Chinese family had taken him in and named him Gansheng. Though the inscription on the bracelet was a mystery, they made his last name Barto. Gansheng Barto, son of Li and Chow Tang. Chow, a retired online learning facilitator, encouraged his adopted son to take courses over the Internet, which Gansheng did, and did well. Within months, he'd passed the exams for his BA in Commercialization and Optimization of the Masses (almost, said Chow, as though he'd already taken the full course of studies in another life). He won a scholarship in the most coveted of all studies, the Get Wealthy In Five Years After Finishing This Program program.

Interviewer: What motivated you to take the program?

Barto: Greed.

Only ten students world-wide were accepted each year and only one or two finished the program. Gansheng finished at the top of the class, specializing in Fast Food Industry Domination.

Interviewer: But a year after graduation, you were nowhere near making a start toward getting wealthy in five years. Your idea for a hickory barbecue huo guo, or hot pot soup, franchise flopped miserably. And...

Barto: Shut up.

It was true though. Every possible fast food concept had been tried from burgers to chicken and pizza to tacos, from drive-through to fly-through for jet packers, from good-for-your-heart-and-soul to damn-the-fat-I'm-hungry, there just wasn't anything left to try, or at least, nothing that Gansheng could put his finger on until he heard of a genetic engineer named John Jonathan Toole who'd been drummed out of the scientific community for trying to clone his own 1960s rock band.

But Toole had a concept for producing fast food that just might work.

Interviewer: It seems an unlikely partnership.

Barto: Not really…I had the business; Toole had the science. And we were both greedy bastards.

After two years of research and finagling to get the venture capital, and another couple of years of research and production, Barto Burger, the world's first cloned food outlet, opened in the center of Shanghai. They'd created the perfect burger and their cloning process allowed them to make infinite copies using burger DNA and a growing solution called The Wash. There were no cooking stoves in the Barto Burger outlets, just microwaves to warm the food. Even the fries were cloned. Boston remembered a telling part of the interview:

Interviewer: It's rumored that you refused to sell a franchise to your adoptive parents. How do you respond to that?

Barto: I have no parents.

Interviewer: I was speaking of Li and Chow…

Barto: Is this interview over?

Interviewer: So, moving on…

Gansheng Barto was a heartless bastard and that was exactly the right nucleus in the driving force for a franchise operation that spread over the surface of the earth like a hungry virus. Barto exploited the post-AIDS baby boom seniors by

20

forcing franchise owners to hire old ladies and dress them up in showgirl costumes to attract a clientele of old men. The women were encouraged to engage in catfights, attacking each other with prosthetic devices, raking each other's faces with their false teeth, and sometimes dropping dead on the job from the excitement. This attracted the jobless youth who cheered when they saw one die because they thought the old ladies were taking jobs away from them. It also prompted elderly men to buy more burgers than they could ever eat.

Interviewer: In the first five years of operation, two hundred and twenty-nine elderly employees of Barto Burger worldwide died on the job of heart attack, stab wounds, concussion, asphyxiation, loss of blood, and severed heads. What seems strange to me about this is that, since your food is cloned and ready to eat as is, why were sharp objects within reach of these people?

Barto: Marketing. It's all in the marketing. No great product was ever greater than its marketing.

And the marketing extended right into the toilets. A plaque on the door of every stall in every Barto Burger outlet in the world read:

Thank you for your deposit.

Your stool and/or urine will be analyzed to determine your culinary preferences.

Please be sure to flush so that we can serve you better.

But it was in the headquarters building, The Spit in Saint, John where Barto Burger International went right over the deep end.

Interviewer: Your employees in Saint John are required to wear robes and hoods. They have to leave their homes and families, live in the headquarters building, and devote their entire lives to Barto Burger. Is there any difference between your staff in Saint John and monks in feudal Europe?

Barto: We let them keep their names.

Interviewer: But...

Barto: We let them keep their names.

Just months ago, the media was rocked again by a story about the Rogers family in Oregon who were refused the body of their son, Carl, after he'd died of a heart attack in his quarters in the Saint John building. Barto Burger kept his body and put it in burial catacombs deep under the building. Carl Rogers had signed a contract giving the company the right to do this. The Rogers family wasn't even invited to the funeral and they were never allowed to visit their son's tomb.

The media blasted Barto.

But now he was a lifeless mass of water and DNA lying on the floor and dripping half-chewed food from his mouth. There was nothing panther-like about him and the only thing chilling about his eyes was their lack of life.

Chapter 6 - Loyalty, Can It Be Bought?

Beaton's beady little eyes were beginning to annoy Boston. The man just stared and stared with his mouth trembling as though he were on the verge of saying something, but nothing came. It gave Boston the creeps. He had to break the silence.

"Who found the body?"

Beaton stared and trembled for a moment before speaking. "Dr. Toole, of course, our chief science officer." He returned to staring mode. Boston waited a moment.

"And?"

"And what, Mr. Jonson?"

Boston took a deep breath. "You're pretty weird, aren't you, Beaton?"

"I beg your...?"

"Tell me about Dr. Toole finding the body. When? How? What was he doing here? Was there anybody else with him? What do you know about Dr. Toole finding the body? Tell me everything."

Beaton's mouth shuddered and his red face flushed deeper. Boston's face remained implacably smug.

"I wouldn't know any of that," said Beaton. "I was merely informed of his findings. When I arrived, he was already gone."

"Then I'll need to speak to him."

"I'm afraid that won't be possible, Mr. Jonson." Beaton spoke like tar pouring. "Dr. Toole and Mr. Barto, as I'm sure you are aware, were close friends, and Dr. Toole was, of course, quite shaken. He retired to his room after receiving a sedative, and he's presently quite asleep."

"Well, I'll have to speak to him as soon as he's *quite* awake in the morning." He turned away from Beaton's stare and walked toward the body. He took out his wallet, flipped it open and punched a button on his wallet phone. A female face appeared on the phone's tiny screen. "I'll need an ambulance and a forensic consultant at the Barto Burger building."

The woman on the screen winked. "On the way." Boston pocketed his wallet and stooped over the body. Barto's stomach bulged like an over-inflated basketball split down the middle, except this basketball bled. Blood soaked the white shirt and blue jacket; it formed a black pool on the floor and had begun to soak into the wrappers before it dried. The packing box beside him said "96 units." Boston figured that meant ninety-six burgers. He looked inside the box. There were only a dozen left.

He turned to Beaton, "These would have been cold when he ate them?"

"Possibly."

"And how did they get here?"

"I wouldn't know."

"Was Mr. Barto in the habit of bringing boxes of cold burgers into this room, sitting on the floor, and eating them until his stomach burst open?"

Beaton glared. "I wouldn't know, Mr. Jonson. That's why you're here."

"I'm here to make a referral, Mr. Beaton. Nothing more."

"And how long will that take, Mr. Jonson?"

"Don't know. Few minutes, few hours. We'll see."

Beaton stared. "Of course. Then you won't be needing me. I have things to which I must attend." He turned and walked toward the door through which Boston had entered. Boston let him leave. He didn't mind people watching him while he worked, but Beaton's stare was too creepy. He bent over the body again, looking closely at the face. Wide bulging eyes, long open mouth, white skin. This man had been horrified before he died. Why would he be afraid if this were a suicide attempt? Did someone force him to eat all those burgers? Was this just an eating binge gone awry?

He looked around the room. The marble statues were nearly as creepy as Beaton's stare. Fog massaged the windows and seemed to absorb whatever dismal light came from the spider-like chandeliers. He wondered how people got up to the balcony that circled the room. No doors. No stairs. No elevators. *Damned elaborate ornament*, he thought.

Time to read the vibrations. He stood erect and closed his eyes as the hooded figures around him looked on silently. He breathed deeply, slowly. He listened to the air. He listened to the spill of blood from the dead man's stomach. He listened to the horror in the man's face. He flared his nostrils and breathed in the terrifying aroma of death. He allowed the texture of events to brush against his soul like seaweed swaying in the ebb and flow of time. He breathed slower, deeper. He held out his hands, palms up, and rubbed his thumbs against his fingertips, trying to stir into wakefulness whatever vibrations slept and dreamed about the last moments of Gansheng Barto's life. Boston left his soul open to their story.

As always, nothing happened.

He turned to one of the hooded figures and said, "The ambulance and a forensics consultant will be here soon. Inform Mr. Beaton that I'll be back tomorrow morning at nine to talk to him and Dr. Toole.

The hood nodded. Boston took one last glance around the room. He wondered about the chair sitting in the center of the room, and he wondered how the hell people were supposed to get up to the wooden balcony that surrounded the room. He walked to the door. Just before he left, he looked back at the dead man and wondered: *Who were you for those first twenty-five years of life? And who were you when you died?*

***

The hand that held the burning pages was steady, resolute, a hand that took care of things and was firm, a hand that committed, just like the hand holding the smoking match. Eyes just as resolute and steady read the words as they burned on the top page:

June 9

I suppose I should have guessed that betrayal might come from the most unlikely corners, but I should expect these things by now-that loyalty cannot be bought, nor can it be trusted when the loyalty is to one such as I. I'll deal with this later, though. In the meantime, my change of character seems to be having the intended effect and I should soon have the rest weeded out...along with my little changeling.

No, Gansheng, loyalty even to one such as you can be bought...temporarily.

Chapter 7 - The Twin Boar Bed and Breakfast

The dining room in the Twin Boar Bed and Breakfast could have been lifted from a Fifteenth Century country road in South Devonshire. And so could Mrs. Orange, proprietor, waitress, housekeeper, laundress, and astounding repository of local history and scuttlebutt. Her skin was as grained and knotted as the wooden floor that held a dozen small tables with half of them occupied by people eating quietly and reading the e-rags, their steady stream of backlit words and images lighting the readers' faces with glowing orange and blue. Boston's wallet was flipped open on the table and he was reading his morning email as Mrs. Orange poured orange juice into his glass.

"Saint John is one of the most historical cities in the world, you know, Mr. Jonson."

Boston nodded as he read the forensic report on Gansheng Barto's death.

"Oldest incorporated city in Canada, you know."

Boston nodded. Reading Forensic Reports 100 had been his worst subject at e-College. All that doctor language and Latin stuff bored the hell out of him. Benny Wisert, the pathologist who'd sent him the report knew this. At the end of the report, he summed it up Boston-style:

He ate himself to death. No signs of foul play - Benny

"First postage stamp album was invented here in...oh, let me see...when did Bobby do that? Oh yes...1853." She finished pouring the juice and stood erect, bringing her height to a dizzying four and a half feet. "It's in the Collector's Club in New York now, you know."

Boston looked at her. Seated, his eyes were on the same level as hers, standing. "What's in New York?" he said.

Mrs. Orange's withered face lit up. "Why, the world's first postage stamp album, Mr. Jonson. Invented right here in Saint John, it was, in 1853."

"You certainly know a lot about the city."

"Lived here all my life, sir. Seen a lot, read a lot."

"Know much about the Barto Burger building?"

The old woman frowned. "We don't talk about that place around her, Mr. Jonson." Orange juice pitcher in hand, she shuffled to the next table.

Boston watched her, wondering just how old she might have been, and what it would be like to have a life that spanned how many generations? He looked back at this email. *No foul play*, he thought. *Just ate himself to death. Why would anyone kill himself that way? Why not shoot himself? Jump off the top of his building? Poison? Smother himself between a pair of large breasts? But he picked what must have been just about the most painful death imaginable. Was he trying to punish himself? Was he trying to make some kind of statement? Or was this something completely different than it looked?*

Chapter 8 - Gargoyles

Even in daylight - or what passed as daylight in a city permanently buried in fog - The Spit was bizarre in a ponderous medieval way, like a great stone relic towering into the misty Twenty-first Century sky. Granite arcades, gargoyle-enshrouded towers, and pinnacled abutments flashed on and off in the roiling clouds of mist. Boston looked down the street. At first, he couldn't see to the end of the block, but then the fog swirled and he could see for two blocks, and the fog swirled again and he could see less than a block.

He'd arrived an hour early so that he could look around on his own, get a feel for the place and the people, maybe even pick up a few vibes. (Well, who knows?) Something moved in the fog to his left, something big moving slow and loud. It was yelling and shaking things at The Spit. It was spitting at The Spit. *Spitters*, thought Boston. One by one, they emerged from the fog; old men with canes, spitting and yelling; young women, pushing baby carriages with one hand, shaking fists with the other; children imitating their parents, yelling words beyond their years and spewing great quantities of white saliva. The crowd passed around Boston, barely noticing him, their hatred focused on the giant structure looming in the fog. And then, as eerily as they appeared, they disappeared, grumbling and mumbling into the vapor on Boston's right.

He looked back at the building. There was something particularly haunting about the Barto

Burger headquarters, something other than the grim stone, the flying buttresses, the sky-stabbing spinnerets, and the lichen-mouthed gargoyles dripping liquefied mist. Boston narrowed his eyes, trying to see the whole of the building as much as it revealed itself in the mist, and within seconds he had it. There was no light coming from inside the building. The stained glass windows were dark under their limestone arches. Even though it was day there was little light under the cloud of fog, but buildings around The Spit-restaurants, stores, and houses-emanated a yellow glow from their windows. Nothing came out of The Spit.

Boston thought about the corporate profile he'd read in his wallet the night before.

Faced with growing competition from a global array of cloned fast food, from cloned pizza and donuts to grown subs and tacos, since the mysterious leak of the highly secret cloning process, the Barto Burger executive has been tight-lipped in recent days. But this is not to say that they appear shaken in the light of dwindling profits and extensive internal problems with supply lines, franchise closures and boycotts by civil rights groups. Indeed, Mackenzie "Mac" Beaton, Senior Vice President of Operations, said in a recent interview: "We have a new technology in development that will ensure our predominance in the industry far into the future."

Mr. Beaton refused to elaborate on the "new technology", and sources inside the organization are saying nothing.

As Boston surveyed the mammoth structure, it seemed no surprise that this would be a place of secrets and silence, and a mystery that drew Boston in like a moth hovering over a camp fire thinking: *I bet I can take it on.*

He walked to the main entrance.

***

High above Boston, in a dark gargoyle-infested corner of the building, a pair of eyes glared at him through a small round window. *Make your referral quickly, fool, and leave with your life.*

Chapter 9 - The Prime Burger

Walking into The Spit, you crossed into a rib-vaulted world of pillars and arches, a world of stained glass and intricately carved wood, where aisles of columns flared upward, forcing chins and eyes up, up and away from the real world and into the dark domes and rafters hundreds of feet above.

Down at the earthly level, a camera flashed. Straight ahead, a young woman wearing a light brown robe and hood led a large group of cell and palmcam-toting Oriental people on a tour. Some of the group regarded Boston suspiciously, eyeing his tangerine hair and the bright Hawaiian shirt. He smiled at them. They looked away. He joined the tour.

"And over here," said the tour guide's singsong voice, "we have the Prime Burger, itself." She waved her arm toward a crystal case, pyramid in shape, with shards of color flickering over its triangular surfaces. "The parent of trillions of flawless burgers around the world." (giggle) Soft light that seemed to originate out of the air inside the case illuminated the unblemished honey-gold top and creamy white edges of the most famous hamburger bun in the history of fast food. There was something liquid and possessing about the bun, a quality that was enough to make you say, "Just the bun, m'am, just the bun." But then the eye moved down to the fixings and meat: opaque onions, ruby tomatoes, lava-thick ketchup, and creamy mayonnaise. And was that a hint of green lettuce leaf poking out just under the rim of the

33

upper bun and over a slathering of bright yellow mustard? It was impossible to tell. It was a mystery, and the mystery was replicated in the billions of Barto Burgers (each a perfect copy of the burger in the case) every year. It was an enigma even more profound than the Mona Lisa smile, only you couldn't eat a smile, and God knows, you could never burp a smile.

Then there was the meat (or what looked like meat since none of it was real), braised and browned and moist, always moist. This was a burger built for endurance. It needed no cold storage and it would sit for a millennium without a sign of mold, spoilage, decay, discoloration, limpness, runniness, tainting, or smelliness. It was immune to time and expiration dates.

"It was created to embody the integration of universal culinary taste," said the tour girl. "The visionaries in our research and development department tried to capture the ultimate spirit of food. They called it the Total Unifying Taste."

A tiny ancient man in the group raised his hand.

"Yes, sir?" said the girl.

"You tell me if it all one part?"

The girl smiled. "Yes, sir. That's exactly right! It's all one piece. You see, instead of cloning cattle and plants, they just cloned the end product, the entire burger." (giggle) The crowd drew closer. "First, they created the Prime Burger." She waved her hand at it again. "Through a series of DNA modifications and combinations-it's all really a mystery to any but a handful of scientists in the world-they made a burger that looks like any other burger, except for being perfect (giggle), but it's all one piece, and every piece tastes like the total burger. Take a bite of the bun and you can taste bun, meat and toppings all at once. The same if you nibble at the meat. It's all one piece and it all tastes the same. The Total Unifying Taste!"

The crowd applauded. The old man smiled wide enough to smooth his wrinkled head into something like a large brass ball with eyes. The tour girl smiled and bowed. The crowd murmured among themselves in Japanese and bowed back to the girl, smiling and nodding. Pictures were taken. Digital video footage was recorded. Notes were made in guidebooks and travel diaries. Observations and opinions were exchanged. Boston was knocked off his feet, sprawling face first into the floor where the cold stone smashed his nose into a bloody mess.

Chapter 10 - Oops

Time and space converged madly around Boston as he lay on the floor, his face pressed against cold stone, nose spurting blood, vision spinning like an out-of-control Frisbee. He breathed deeply and tried to relax, to tap into the vibrations of this strange situation. But, nothing happened, at least not in the way of vibrations. However, when he turned his head and looked up, he faced the most beautiful woman he'd ever seen. Her white robe glowed all the whiter for the deep black of her shoulder-length hair, so deep it threatened to absorb the color out of his eyes. His head still spun like a Frisbee. The woman's hair looped over one big brown eye with a brow that reached into forever, her cheeks glowed cheerily red, her full lips curled mirthfully, almost sarcastically, and she said, "Oops!"

Oops, thought Boston, *she wears red cheeks oops and I said oops and I ask her with my eyes oops again and oops and if I asked her oops to say oops as I put my arms around her and draw her down to me oops so I can...*

"Ouch!" yelled Boston as the dark-haired woman stepped on his fingers.

"Oh, I'm so sorry," she said. "And right after knocking you down." Her mouth, still curled mirthfully, curled further, as though she were about to start laughing. That was all

Boston needed. With his sore fingers over his nose, blood oozing between them, he laughed. The woman looked at him quizzically at first, thought a moment and then she too laughed. The members of the tour group looked first at Boston shedding swatches of liquid red over an already blaring Hawaiian hula-hula shirt, then at the woman in the white robe, her hood down, her black hair absorbing their irises, and as one they burst out laughing. The worry dropped off the tour guide's face and she giggled.

"Oops!" said Boston, holding his bloodied hand out toward the woman. She nearly doubled over. "Oops!" she shrieked.

"Boston Jonson," said Boston, his hand still out, propped on one knee.

"Marlee Dunn," said the woman. "Do I really have to shake that?" She pointed at his bloodied hand. Boston gazed at it like something that didn't belong at the end of his arm and cupped it around his nose. He stood up, wavering slightly.

"Kind of hoping you'd kiss it better," he said.

"In your dreams, CI guy."

"You know I'm a CI?"

"Are you kidding? You're in the e-rags all the time. Boston Jonson making this famous referral, that ground-breaking recommendation, dishing out mind-boggling criminal consulting from New York to Vancouver."

Hearing this, the tour group drew closer, pictures were taken, digital video recorded, notes taken, and smiles wrapped around a dozen Asian faces.

"I'm really sorry," said Marlee. "I'm probably the clumsiest ass you'll ever meet." She turned to the tour guide. "Call the infirmary and say I'm bringing in someone with a nose injury, heavy bleeding." She turned back to Boston. "Follow me." Boston looked quickly at the tour group and half raised his other hand. They waved and nodded and bowed and smiled. Boston followed Marlee toward a large wooden door. He looked down at the curve under Marlee's robe and thought, *Nothing clumsy about that ass*.

Chapter 11 - Never-ending Staircase

They'd been climbing a circular staircase for several minutes, its stone steps newly ancient with simulated use.

"You didn't miss much on the tour," said Marlee. "It's all a pile of crap for the tourists and the corporate wannabes. But the aura around that damned piece of fake ticky-tacky is very convincing. One old guy on crutches got about five feet away from it, threw down his crutches and started walking again."

"Sounds like a convincing pile of crap."

"Oh, it is. The marketing budget for this bunch is more than the gross national product for most countries. But even the Prime, when you think about it, is all hype. It was all just as much show business as it was science. Once they had the basic burger cloning process perfected, they brought in teams of make-up artists, vibration analysts, graphic designers, photographers, landscapers, architects, psychologists, nutritionists, packaging specialists, interior decorators and a bunch of others. They were told to make the burger look perfect, something that would appeal to everybody. The nutritionists said, 'Take out the pickle. Nobody really wants a pickle in the perfect burger.' So they took out the pickle. The rest of them studied videos of people eating junk food. They studied their faces as they ate and they counted how many times they chewed each bite. They even recorded the slurping and munching sounds and compared them with facial expressions."

Boston wondered if the stairs eventually ended somewhere on the roof, or maybe in one of the domed towers he'd seen through the fog. He worried that he might bleed to death before he reached the infirmary, but the curvy sway of Marlee's robe drew him upward through the winding corridor.

"They fed all the information into some kind of nuclear clock computer that crunched digits in some other dimension. Then they added entire libraries of information on nutrition, marketing, taste studies, consumer eating and spending habits and a whole bunch more. All this research and studying culminated in a single image. It was an image of the Prime Burger, the thing you were just looking at downstairs. Then they modified the DNA in the prototype clone to produce the Prime. And all the billions, make that trillions, of Barto burgers that have been eaten all around the planet in the last few decades, all came from the DNA in that single chunk of junk in the pyramid case."

"Fascinating," said Boston, staring at Marlee's butt.

"They had another version for a while, a health food burger with just one calorie. One calorie in the entire burger, and not a single gram of fat! And best of all, it tasted exactly like its fat-loaded twin. I mean it. The taste in those things doesn't come from the foodstuff. It comes from a DNA-encoded taste enzyme. They both shared exactly the same enzyme."

Boston looked at his hand. Blood was beginning to clot between his fingers.

"But people hated it! They hated the healthy burger. Said it didn't taste right, that it didn't taste like a real burger. As if even the original burger was real. Nobody would buy it. They took it off the market. People don't eat fast food to get healthy. Even the cloned fries are bred to be artery clogging. But the pop's not cloned. It's still the over-carbonated watered-down sugar-drenched chemical-tasting sludge that's in every fast-food joint on earth."

Boston noticed that she did something surreptitiously with her right arm and then tilted her head back. *Taking a little morning nip?*

"How's your nose?" she asked.

"I think most of my blood supply is drying on my hand."

Marlee looked back and Boston held up his bloodied hand. His nose, mouth, chin and shirt were equally gory.

"I'm so sorry, Mr. Jonson. I'm such a..."

"Boston."

"Pardon?"

"Call me Boston. And don't sweat it. It's not often that beautiful women knock me down, smash my face, step on my fingers and then make me climb a thousand flights of stairs while I bleed to death. I think I could learn to like this."

He watched her neck turn red. "We'll be there in a minute," she said. "Again...I'm..."

"Buy me lunch and we're square."

41

She flung a look back at him and smiled. "You're on." Then she missed a step and tumbled downward, banging the back of her head heavily into Boston's nose.

Chapter 12 - Something To Think About

There seemed to be something inappropriate about the infirmary doctor wearing a red robe, especially in a room that smelled like rubbing alcohol and looked like something out of a B grade Frankenstein movie, but there he stood, red robe and all, staring at Boston's bloody nose, saying, "Is that real blood?"

"Yes, Doc. In fact, I think that's the last of it. The rest is in the staircase."

The doctor's face was long and emotionless inside the red hood. His eyes were the color of boredom. "Perhaps we'll lay you at the bottom, run a tube up the steps, and give you a transfusion of your own blood."

Boston looked into the man's eyes. They were blank. His flat lips neither smiled nor frowned. It was impossible to tell if he was being funny or sarcastic. Boston was not about to be intimidated by an enigmatic face. "Perhaps I'll lay you down and..."

"This is Mr. Jonson," interjected Marlee. "The famous CI. I knocked him down in the main hall and...well...smashed his nose."

"Marlee, you bring me more business than flu, cholesterol, and VD," said he doctor, dispassionately. "I'm surprised the people who underwrite our insurance plan don't send assassins after you."

"It was just an accident," said Boston.

"It always is," said the doctor. "But I suppose I should look at your nose, Mr. Jonson. I'm Doctor Rains. Have a seat." He pointed to a gurney. Boston made his way unsteadily to it and pushed himself up onto a tightly stretched white sheet.

Rains pulled on a pair of clear rubber gloves, fussed around in a cabinet and took out several small boxes. "I suppose you're here to refer on Gansheng Barto's death," he said as he lay the boxes on the gurney beside Boston. He studied the gory nose from several angles and said, "Ah, yes. Looks like you're going to have a sore snout for a while." Boston winced as the doctor poked and pinched his nose. "Nothing broken. Marlee, you're losing your touch."

Marlee frowned and stuck her tongue out at him.

He washed the blood away from Boston's face with an alcohol-soaked swab. "Bleeding seems to have stopped, Mr. Jonson. Maybe you did leave it all in the staircase." He finished cleaning and threw the blood-soaked swab across the room into a plastic bucket.

"Nice shot," said Boston.

"With Marlee around, I get lots of practice," said Rains dryly.

Marlee flicked her tongue at him again.

"Too early to tell if you're going to have a shiner, but I wouldn't be surprised. Most likely your left eye, maybe both. You might also experience some light-headedness and disorientation. This will pass when you distance yourself from Marlee."

44

Boston started to laugh but checked himself when Marlee shot him an evil glare. "Thanks, Doc. Mind if I wash my hands in your sink?"

"Feel free," said Rains. Boston slipped off the gurney and walked to the sink. "He was a vegetarian, you know."

"I beg your pardon?" said Boston.

"Barto. He was a vegetarian. Wouldn't touch meat for the world, cloned or otherwise. Strange that he would eat himself to death on hamburgers."

"You're sure of this?"

"Besides working the infirmary, I was his personal physician. Gansheng Barto was a vegetarian."

Boston thought about this as he washed his hands and Doctor Rains shook Marlee's hand and thanked her for keeping him in business.

Chapter 13 - Klutz

The tour group was gone from the main hall and the Prime Burger lay under its crystalline pyramid unappreciated, unworshipped, unawe-inspiring, and completely unaware of any of this, being, after all, nothing more than reconstituted DNA.

"Your nose is blue," said Marlee.

"Thanks," said Boston. "I'll keep that in mind every minute for the rest of the day. How're my eyes?"

"Blue. Sort of."

"I'm a matching set. Sort of."

Marlee laughed deeply and maybe a little too carelessly. Boston wondered just how many nips she had in the course of a day.

"I'm a klutz," she said.

"What?"

"I'm a klutz. And I'm sorry for making your nose blue and then stomping your fingers. Doc Rains is right. I keep him in business. I'm a klutz."

"Well, if you weren't a klutz I wouldn't be having lunch with you. Will I survive lunch?"

"Promise. See you at noon. In the cafeteria." She pointed toward a door on the side of the hall. The neon sign with CAFETERIA on it looked strangely out of place in a building that Boston only just noticed had no other signs. Nothing was labeled. Even the reception desk to which Marlee had taken him was just an old wooden desk with a somber-faced robed woman sitting behind it. There was nothing on the desktop.

Marlee smiled and walked away. Boston stared after her. *Definitely nothing clumsy about that ass.*

He walked to the reception desk and the somber woman looked up at him. In spite of the somberness, she was beautiful. "Yes?" Beautiful and stern-voiced.

"My name is Boston Jonson. I..."

"Oh yes, you." She touched a wooden panel on her desktop and a screen appeared. She looked at the screen and frowned. "You're half an hour late."

Boston pointed to his blue nose and said, "Accident. I was here early but I had a run-in with one of your employees."

"Marlee Dunn?"

"Yes. How...?"

"Just a moment." She touched another panel and a door opened about twenty feet behind the reception desk. A tall, brown-robed figure emerged from the door and walked up to Boston. From inside the hood a deep voice commanded, "Follow me, Mr. Jonson." As they walked away from the desk, Boston noticed that the woman was staring directly ahead, motionless, and seemingly unaware that she'd been talking to anyone just seconds before.

Chapter 14 - Thumbs Up

"What happened to your nose?" said Mackenzie Beaton, enunciating each word vowel-by-vowel, syllable-by-syllable, consonant-by-consonant, staring. "It's blue."

"So I've been told," said Boston.

Beaton's office was much the same as the rest of The Spit: stone walls and floors, aged wood furniture, stained glass windows and cumbersome doors-a slice of feudal European churchdom plopped into the second millennium.

"You realize, of course, that you're half an hour late?" Staring, mouth trembling.

"You're just as weird in the day as you are at night, aren't you?" Staring right back.

Beaton took a deep breath and let it out the same way he talked, a slow don't-mess-with-me-because-I-can-give-you-a-world-of-pain release of breath. Boston was unruffled. He'd been here before, many times. People like Mackenzie Beaton with his red face, his stare, and his intimidating size that intimidated anyone within intimidation distance were fuel for Boston's outrageous Hawaiian shirts, manna for his long tangerine hair, and pure inspiration for his screw-you attitude. He met Beaton eye-to-eye and waited out the long breath. Beaton caved. "I assume you have questions, Mr. Jonson. Perhaps you should just ask and I can address them. Then you can make your referral and go on to your next assignment."

"Sounds like you're trying to get rid of me, but that's OK, Beaton. I'm used to it." Boston took his wallet from his shirt pocket. It had a recording device that converted sound signals directly into written documents that he could print out that evening at the bed and breakfast. "What was Mr. Barto's state of mind in the last few weeks?"

"I'm afraid you would have to ask him that, Mr. Jonson. I've never actually been inside his mind."

Boston stared deeper into Beaton's eyes. "Did he seem...distraught? Nervous? Depressed? Afraid? Did he...act different...than normal?"

"No."

"Thank you. Was he under pressure?"

"He was, of course, quite hated by the many thousands of people he obliterated in this rise to power, Mr. Jonson. Our competition has been gaining on us and stealing our secrets. Profits are down and costs are up. Scandals about employee treatment have been giving us a black eye. Our entire corporate culture is under public scrutiny. But no, I wouldn't say that Mr. Barto was under any pressure that one would consider abnormal."

"You're not going to help me, are you?"

"I'll cooperate with you in any way I can."

"When was the last time you saw Mr. Barto?"

"Yesterday."

"Yesterday?"

"That's correct."

"OK then, Beaton, exactly what time yesterday? Where? And what did you and Mr. Barto talk about?"

"Eleven AM. In this office. The weather."

"The weather?"

"He remarked that it seemed a bit foggy."

"It's been a bit foggy for over thirty years in this city."

"Then, of course, that would be considered an astute observation."

Boston pocketed his wallet. "You know, *of course*, that refusing to cooperate with a CI referral consultation is a criminal offense punishable by up to twenty hours of community service?"

"I didn't realize the penalty was quite that harsh. Is there anything else you want from me, Mr. Jonson?"

"As a matter of fact, yes. Someone from your staff who can show me around the building, introduce me to the people I have to talk to, expedite things a little, someone other than you."

A chill flowed into Beaton's stare. He walked to his wooden desk, its surface cracked and crannied like something out of a junk shop. He pressed his thumb on the desktop. A minute later, the door opened and a woman wearing a light blue robe walked in. She held a porcelain coffee mug in her left hand.

"Mr. Jonson, Bethany Moore," said Beaton. "Miss Moore is one of our directors of public relations. She will, of course, be happy to guide you through your referral research."

The woman extended her right hand and Boston shook it. Like Marlee, she wore her hood down. Unlike Marlee, she wore her chestnut brown hair in a ponytail that flicked upward at the top of her neck. There was something energetic about it, like a race horse at the gate. Her face was slim, her nose long, and her eyes brown and sparkling. There was also something metallically cold in her eyes that he couldn't put his finger on. "I've heard a lot about you, Mr. Jonson. You're somewhat of a legend."

He immediately liked her.

"I do my best," he said.

"Miss Moore," said Beaton, "I'd like you to be Mr. Jonson's guide while he gathers information for his referral. See what you can do to cut through red tape for him and, of course, make all the appropriate introductions."

She smiled and looked at Boston. There was a glowing quality in the whiteness and dimpledness of her smile that tugged gently at Boston's heart, but when she said, "I would be honored, Mr. Jonson," Boston noticed that she wasn't looking at him. She was looking somewhere to his left. Boston glanced around. It was an ancient wooden cabinet with mirrored doors. He could see his reflection and Bethany's. She was looking at herself, up and down, squinting her eyes slightly, assessing and evaluating. And then, finally, she approved and said, "Where would you like to start?"

"With the last person to see Mr. Barto alive, Ms Moore."

"Call me Bethany. Please." She looked questioningly at Beaton.

"That would, of course, be Dr. Toole," said Beaton.

"Of course," said Bethany. "This way, Mr. Jonson."

"Boston. Please." And he turned to face straight into Beaton's stare. "By the way, don't you think it's

51

strange that Mr. Barto would eat himself to death on hamburgers? Him being a vegetarian and all."

"I wouldn't know anything about that," said Beaton.

"Right. Of course. I'll be in touch." Beaton's stare was stonewall cold as Boston turned and walked out of the office with a new robe curving and swaying in front of him. He glanced back quickly at Beaton just before he went out the door. Beaton's eyebrows narrowed slightly and he turned away.

He knows something, thought Boston.

Chapter 15 - Bethany's Little Slip

"What floor is this?" asked Boston.

They were in a hall that stretched for at least three hundred feet with six huge multi-paned windows every fifty feet emitting dismal light. The ceiling must have been at least sixty feet high.

"We're on the fifth floor, Mr. Jonson," said Bethany. "This is the South wing of the building. It overlooks the harbor."

They passed one of the giant windows. A cloud of fog pushed and eddied against the glass. "I see," said Boston. "And this is the business wing, where the administration offices are located? And by the way, it's Boston. Please."

"Exactly. In fact, all the rooms above ground are either business-related or accommodations. Everything else is underground. That's where we're going now." She sipped from her cup.

"You always carry coffee around with you?"

"Keeps me perky, Mr. Jonson, a big plus in my work." As she spoke, she looked past him again. He followed her gaze to her reflection in the window. He turned to face her. "We're going underground?"

"That's where the labs and production lines are, and that's where Dr. Toole works." She suddenly turned to her left and stopped. A section of wall opened into an elevator.

"Where did that come from?" said Boston.

Bethany made a laugh-like sound, something forced and chopped, but Boston could forgive that: the dimples were completely natural. "A concealed sensor scanned my eyes and opened the doors. All the elevators to the lower levels are hidden and accessed only by people whose eyes match their security clearance rating. Your eyes were just scanned as well, and you've been added to the system with a referral level access appropriate to the Access to Referral Law."

"Very smooth," said Boston. "How long have you had this system in place?"

"It was implemented right after the cloning process was leaked."

"Just how serious was that?" asked Boston as he entered the elevator.

"It was our competitive advantage, Mr. Jonson. We didn't need cooks and ovens. Do you have any idea how low your overhead sinks in the food industry when you serve food that never spoils? And people just liked the idea. It put us light years ahead of everyone else and made us the biggest and the best. But as soon as the secret was out, everyone was cloning their food: pizzas, potato chips, tacos, hot dogs. Not to mention all the other burger chains."

Boston noticed something just under her voice, something like anger or disappointment, or both. He couldn't put his finger on it. Then, in a wink, her face brightened. The walls in the elevator were mirrored and Bethany was busy taking in her image reflected thousands of times in lines of images reaching deep into all four walls.

"Yeah, that sounds serious all right. But I heard that Mr. Beaton had some new technology or other that was going to put the company back on track."

He could almost feel her stiffen. She looked at his reflected image, right into his reflected image eyes. "You'll have to talk to Mr. Beaton about that. I wouldn't know anything…"

"Whoa. I'm sorry. It was just something I read. I didn't realize that it was unbroachable."

Bethany rolled her eyes. "That's not what I meant either, Mr. Jonson. I just meant that I wouldn't be able to give you an accurate assessment of Mr. Beaton's plans. You would have to talk to him."

"Sure, I'll do that later. Did you know Mr. Barto?"

The suddenness of the question caught her. She thought a moment, looking herself up and down in the mirrors. "Not well. He kept mostly to himself. Stayed in his rooms most of the time. He didn't like public exposure." Again, something in her voice.

"Did he seem happy?"

She gave his reflected eyes a what-are-you-crazy-or-something look and said, "You'll have to ask Mr. Beaton that, or maybe Dr. Toole could tell you. He was very close to Mr. Barto and he wasn't happy about this happening again." She froze. Her mouth clamped shut. She looked directly at the mirror, expressionless.

"What happening again?" said Boston.

Though her face was frozen, the fury of thought was obvious in her eyes, looking for a way out, and finding none, she said, "Something…something to do with our cloning process, I think. I'm not sure. It's highly confidential and I really shouldn't have mentioned it. I'll see what I can find out for you if you think it might have a bearing on your referral."

"Thanks. I appreciate that." *Cloning process my ass*, thought Boston. The elevator doors slid open. *Something linked directly to Barto's death happened and she knows what it is and it's got her spooked as hell*.

But all thoughts of Barto's death and the spooked woman evaporated from his mind as he stared between the open doors and into a scene as amazing as it was disturbing.

"Welcome to The Crib," said Bethany.

Beyond the open doors a sight as amazing as it was disturbing erased the death of magnates and beautiful spooked women from Boston's thoughts.

Chapter 16 - The Crib

The "Crib" spread for over a mile through the granite under-core of the city. Slabs of jagged natural rock jutted out like massive teeth biting out of the walls-part of an underground historical protection program dreamed up by some city councilor to somehow mollify opposition to the building, which would ensure a big kickback to his contracting company. Thousands of long tables with exact rows of Petrie dishes formed lines stretching into the underground distance. Stone columns flared into a complex rib-vaulted ceiling. Stained glass windows with vague motifs lined the high gray walls, their artificial backlight casting a warm haze over the strange room, a quiet light that might have said, "Hush, now, sleep and don't be afraid."

Boston looked closely at the Petrie dishes on a nearby table. In the center of each was a small brown lump.

"Baby burgers," said Bethany. "This is where we grow the replicas of the Prime." She sipped from her cup.

Boston looked around. There must have been tens of thousands of them. "All in this room?"

"No, there's hundreds more all over the world."

"Hundreds," he said, nodding his head once. "Still, it seems like a lot of work to make burgers instead of just frying them up."

Bethany gave him the oh-c'mon-now eye squint. "It takes years to grow a cow, seasons to grow grains and vegetables, weeks or months to harvest and process before you have something to fry and serve up. Here…" She pointed an arc around the rows of tables. "… we grow the whole thing is just three days."

Boston nodded. "Cool."

Silent figures in hooded robes wandered down the aisles between the rows of tables. They stopped and examined dishes, made notes on clipboards, and moved to the next table. The air carried an indefinable aroma that was at once sweet and sour, like old air from an inner tube sandwiched between layers of a saltwater breeze. It was the kind of air to confuse even the most discerning nose. But even in the warmth and the soft light from the stained glass windows high in the stone walls, the room sent a chill racing through that place where Boston stored his life breath. He noticed a low humming sound and a light vibration traveling through the stone floor. He looked down and saw metal pipes running under the tables.

Bethany, following his gaze, said, "They carry the Wash, the nutrient solution that feeds the growing burgers. Smaller pipes under the tables branch out into the bottoms of the growing dishes and pump in the exact same amount of fluid at the exact same time three times a day."

Feeds the growing burgers? thought Boston, and he felt another chill. He nodded.

"In fact," added Bethany, "they're getting lunch as we speak."

"Lunch for supper," said Boston.

Bethany gave him a puzzled look. *She's a beautiful woman*, he thought, *but weird*. Then he thought of something. "Shouldn't we be wearing masks or something, you know, so the burgers don't get infected with germs?"

Bethany smiled. "As I said before, these burgers won't spoil. They're genetically engineered to resist any kind of infection. They're almost like a disinfectant when it comes to germs and viruses, but they're completely safe for human consumption."

"Maybe your scientists should look at doing the same for humans."

"Maybe someday they will."

Another chill.

They walked into the rows of tables toward an island of desks and computers deep in the cavernous room. "So," said Boston, "how is it done? I mean, without giving any trade secrets that haven't already been given away, how do you clone a hamburger?"

Bethany walked in front of him, and Boston, realizing the futility of resisting one's natural proclivities, checked out her butt. He found it nicely shaped, but less relaxed than Marlee's-less sway and swagger. Boston liked sway and swagger in a woman. Maybe Bethany was afraid that she would spill her coffee if she gave vent to the natural movements of her buttocks. Whatever, Boston was still impressed by her form. Anything that could look that good under an ankle-length robe had to possess great artistic merit.

"Tell you what, Mr. Jonson. Take your eyes off my ass and I'll tell you about the cloning process."

Boston looked up. *How did she know?* He looked on the tabletops. Petrie dishes. Glass Petrie dishes with reflective surfaces. Not much of a mirror, but still a mirror. This woman was good at finding her reflection, and anyone else's.

"Thank you, Mr. Jonson."

"Boston."

"I won't bore you with a lot of jargon about polymerase chain reactions, Weismann's Hypothesis, recombinant DNA, the four nucleotide bases: adenine, thymine, cytosine, and guanine. I've never understood any of that, and I have a Masters of Business Aesthetics. Besides, we've gone light years ahead of all that. One of the researchers once told me that DNA produces RNA and then RNA produces protein. I don't know what that means, but this process is called the Central Dogma. That's all I have to know. It's mysterious. Does that answer your question, Mr. Jonson?"

"Mysteriously, no. But..."

As they passed through an intersection of aisles, a man in a white robe caught Boston's eye. He chewed nervously on a toothpick sticking out of his mouth. He started to walk toward Boston but seemed to change his mind and turn away. Then he turned quickly and started toward Boston again. Bethany turned her head toward him and he stopped at a table and pretended to examine a clone baby snoozing quietly in its Petrie dish. "Well, don't worry. There's the man, just up ahead, who can answer all your questions."

Boston turned his head away from the man with the toothpick and looked ahead, past Bethany.

At the edge of the island of desks and computers, stood a short bald-headed man wearing round eyeglasses and a white robe. He appeared to have something intangible surrounding him, as though he emanated a force that made the air all around him shake. Or maybe it was just that Boston had seen his picture a thousand times in the webloids and e-rags. He looked back at the man with the toothpick but he was gone.

"Mr. Jonson, this is Dr. John Jonathan Toole."

***

Forests had been ravaged and bandwidth depleted to provide the mediaocracized public with stories about the strangest personality ever to bonk heads with the Paparazzi-Dr. John Jonathan Toole, or as the media dubbed him, Dr. John.

A masters graduate from the Virtual School of Genetics and Bio-Probabilities at the age of ten, Toole breezed into the world's leading doctoral program in applied genetics while simultaneously heading up the applied genetics research division of the world's largest bio-engineering firm, AppliedGenTechSolutions Corporation. He loved his academic work in spite of the endless arguments with his learning facilitators over foolish things like ethics and scientific responsibility, but he hated his corporate work even though ethics and scientific responsibility were never an issue. There was only one concern: money, and though there seemed to be a bottomless well of it, the well dried quickly when the corporate bean-counters and decision-makers failed to see the practical application, and therefore profitability, in Toole's outrageous ideas.

Strange as it seemed to him, they weren't about to fund a ten year project to use DNA from dead rock stars to create a sixties rock band with Jim Morrison on vocals, Jimi Hendrix on lead guitar, Otis Redding on bass, Joe Cocker (who claimed to still be alive, but nobody believed him) on tambourines-and on drums, why none other than Dr. John Jonathan Toole who, once the band was formed, genuinely intended to take drumming lessons.

He had one idea that interested them, and that one idea was all that kept him on the payroll.

Dr. John Jonathan Toole believed that it was possible to take DNA from various sources and combine it to form something that would equal the sum total of the combination DNA. They gave him a year. After two years, he went to them with a plan to take DNA from all the base ingredients-such as cows, mustard plants, tomatoes, cucumbers, onions, and a huge array of chemicals and compounds-and create a hamburger that could be cloned countless times. This wasn't exactly what they had in mind. In fact, by this time, nobody knew what to expect from Toole.

They fired him.

Someone in the personnel department leaked the firing to the media. Overnight, Dr. John Jonathan Toole was a media sensation. Paparazzi popped out of his closets, microphones turned up in his toilet; camera flashes blinded him when he opened his refrigerator door-more people listened to his phone calls than to radio stations. For months, his picture was everywhere -short, bald, rotund and spooky in round glasses, headlined, DR. JOHN. What the world called him now. Nerds everywhere grew v-shaped goatees. He received offers from Hollywood and from game and talk shows, from NetTV, eProdRadio, EPrintMag and WristNews. He received a notice from the post office to bring in a truck and pick up his snail mail. He received invitations to speak at SciFi conventions and rock revivals. He received a bill from his Internet provider for the purchase, installation and maintenance of a separate server to handle his email.

One of those emails was from Gansheng Barto. He offered to supply funding to perfect the process for cloning hamburgers and then partner with him in the world's first cloned fast food franchise. Barto didn't care what Toole did in his free time. He could resurrect entire symphony orchestras and all the bands and the audience from Woodstock. He would have all the money and privacy he needed. Toole returned his message:

From: morrisonhotel@rockbandsalive.com
To: ganshengbarto@bartosmoney.com
Sent:
Subject: Re: Proposition
And chicks, too?
To which Barto replied:
From: ganshengbarto@bartosmoney.com
To: morrisonhotel@rockbandsalive.com
Sent:
Subject: Re: Proposition

Does the term 'up to your ears in tits and ass' mean anything to you?

Dr. John Jonathan Toole accepted Gansheng Barto's offer, and the two went on to become the wealthiest men in the world. But Toole never did get any chicks. He was just too nerdy.

Chapter 17 - Stir Lightly

Dr. John Jonathan Toole blinked incessantly. He could have been twenty-five, he could have been fifty-five; his pupils were so dilated that he had no irises, it was impossible to tell what color his eyes were. He wore leather sandals with socks-socks with holes in them. But the aura of energy about him was intense, high-strung and metabolically similar to the boundless energy surrounding a gerbil.

Boston reached out his hand to shake, but Toole stood with his hands clasped in front of him and said in a squeaky voice, "Hey, your effin' nose is blue." (blink blink)

"Dr. John, I presume," said Boston.

Toole scowled. Boston smiled sardonically.

"Oh my god," said Bethany. "Your nose *is* blue!"

"Kind of you to notice," said Boston, still eye-to-eye with Toole.

"What happened?" said Bethany.

"Marlee Dunn," said Boston.

Bethany opened her mouth and nodded. "Well then, Mr. Jonson, you're lucky to be alive."

Boston and Toole were still eye-locked, Boston poker-faced, Toole scowling and blinking. Boston wondered if burrowing into each other's eyes was some kind of pastime with the senior management at Barto Burger. He decided to break the silence. "Don't like to be called Dr. John do you, Doctor?"

"That's really effed and, like, unprofessional. And effin' insulting. What're you here for?"

"I'm the CI on Mr. Barto's death."

Suddenly Toole's face lightened and his small mouth stretched into a very gerbil-like smile over the small v of his goatee. "The CI? Boston Jonson? (blink blink) *The*, like, Boston Jonson, CI?"

Boston found himself beginning to like Toole, weird or not. "That's right Dr. Toole. And…"

"Man, like, I've read all your referrals! The Kilburn Blind Man murder referral was, like, pure effin' genius. Thirty naked pagan women? Effin' A, man! Where'd you get the idea? How'd you make that effin' connection?"

"Just popped up. The way things happen sometimes. You were the last person to see Mr. Barto alive?"

Toole's smile stretched further. "Effin' A! (blink blink) Get right into it! So this is, like, how you do it. Like, effin' James Bond and Sam Spade-drop in and stir the crap! Man, I love it! Whaddaya want from me, man. Can I call you Boston?"

"Boston's fine. You were the last one to see Mr. Barto alive?"

"Effin' right I was. Left him around eight. He was, like, all mellow and happy. Been that way for the last few weeks. How am I doing?"

Boston, flattered or not, held on to his poker face. "You're doing great. He was in a good mood?"

"Effin' mellow yellow, man. For the last three weeks, anyway. Like Scrooge after the ghosts. Much as I loved the guy, he used to be like one of the biggest pricks in the world. Would've sold his mother for a few lines of corporate intel if he thought it would give him an effin' five dollar edge on one of his competitors. How am I doing?" (blink blink)

"Great. What caused the change in heart?"

Toole shrugged. "Who knows, man. Happened right out of the blue, you know, like, right out of the blue. One day he was planning to..." Suddenly he stopped smiling and glanced at Bethany, who appeared to have stopped breathing.

"He was planning to...?" said Boston.

"I think Dr. Toole was referring to the new technology," said Bethany. "As I said, you'll have to talk to Mr. Beaton about that."

New technology my ass, thought Boston. *They're hiding something.* He turned to face Toole. "Bethany was saying that you might be able to explain the cloning process to me."

Toole relaxed. Bethany's shoulders dropped slightly. Toole clapped his hands together. "We, like, grew the perfect hamburger through the use of DNA manipulation and nano-technology. Used trans-dimensional computing. Then we cloned it, over and over. We did the same with fries and the same with our whole effin' breakfast menu." He pointed around the giant room. "And here's how we do it. (blink blink) But then our effin' competition stole it from us, and they started doing it. Now everybody's doing it. But we're..." He stopped again, glanced at Bethany and then looked back at Boston.

"But we're...?" prompted Boston.

"This time, the effin' competition's gonna have to do their own R&D," said Toole.

"Sure. I understand. No big deal. Are you really trying to clone a sixties rock band, Doctor?"

In an instant, Boston Jonson, CI, much as he liked to be adored and idolized, lost another fan. Toole narrowed his eyes as though aiming something deadly from the depths of his subconscious directly between Boston's eyes. *You said it, bud, drop right in and stir the shit.*

Chapter 18 - Playing the Game

"Mr. Jonson," said Bethany peevishly. "Do you really think that someone who could create all of this…" She waved her arm in an arc to take in the thousands of tables of Petrie dishes lined up like armies of the future in the fast food war. "…would waste his time on something as ridiculous as a cloned rock and roll band?"

Toole glowered at her. Bethany clamped her mouth.

"I see," said Boston. "Just a lot of media hype."

"Uh, yes," said Bethany.

Toole was back to staring at Boston. He nodded slightly to agree with Bethany. "And what the eff's that got to do with your referral, Jonson?" (blink)

Jonson? Yep, lost another fan. "Nothing, Doctor. Just curiosity. Did Beaton and Mr. Barto agree on the new technology?"

"They did until…" Toole shut up again.

"Mr. Jonson," said Bethany. "If you want information about the new technology…"

"I know, I know, talk to Beaton." Still looking into Toole's eyes, Boston said, "But I think it's safe to assume, that being the head of research, you would be in charge of the new technology…"

"Mr. Jonson!"

Boston turned to Bethany and shrugged. "Right. Talk to Beaton. Talk to Dr. Joh…Dr. Toole about…about…well, Doctor…what *should* we talk about? First Mr. Barto is a bloodless bastard, then he's a reformed Scrooge who's planning something to do with a new secret technology, and then he's dead. Now, what would *you* like to talk about?"

Toole smiled, turned his back on Boston and marched away, followed by three somber figures wrapped in robes.

"Maybe we'll talk later," Boston called after him.

Toole stopped, half turned, blink blinked, and continued walking.

Boston turned to Bethany. "There was a man working in the aisle we just came down. He was wearing a white robe, chewing a toothpick. Do you know who he is?"

"There's over a thousand people working in this building in a dozen different departments, and with the robes, most of them look alike." She looked at him solemnly, almost impatiently, as though he were wasting her time and she'd had about all she needed of that. She obviously wanted to ditch him and get to, maybe, a room full of mirrors. Boston could play that game.

"Let's go back to the big checker board and see what we can stir up there."

70

Chapter 19 - Missing Pages, Missing Years

"A room this big..." Boston looked around the massive room with the checker board floor. Since nothing but fogged light entered through the tall windows, it looked as eerie and puzzling as it had the night before. "And with the exception of a balcony that nobody can get to, and a bunch of weird statutes stuck up against the walls, all he has in this room is a single chair." He touched the brown leather of the chair, dark like unsweetened chocolate. "And not even an Ottoman." The chair's back was straight and high. "Not exactly my idea of a comfy place to while away the evening."

"Mr. Barto rarely had time for relaxation," said Bethany. "Barto Burger is more than just a company. It's more like a holy empire of fast food." Something racing around in her eyes caught Boston's attention. It was something like excitement, though her face was expressionless. Maybe it was awe. She lifted the coffee mug to her lips and sipped with a faint slurping sound. Maybe it was just his imagination.

The spot where they'd found Barto had been whisked clean of death. There wasn't a trace of food wrappings, half chewed burgers, or the blood-and-food-soaked body. But the statues winked with white eyes as though they knew what awful thing had happened in this room just hours ago. Boston put both his hands on the back of the chair and faced the windows. "What do you suppose he saw as he sat in this chair? What happened as he sat here that ultimately led to his death?"

Bethany shrugged her shoulders slowly. "You think that sitting in the chair had something to do with Mr. Barto's death?"

"That's exactly what I mean. One night, he sat in this chair and something changed him. One night be became a different man and the new man had no place in this room. So he died."

"I don't have a clue what you're talking about, Mr. Jonson."

"Neither do I." He shrugged. "Just throwing it out there."

"They've taken away the body and cleaned up the mess. They have holographic reconstructions of it all. Do you really need anything more in this room, Mr. Jonson?"

Boston raised a hand. "Humor me, Bethany. I'd like to try something." He sat in the chair.

He looked straight out the window, focusing his eyes deep into the cloud of fog. He slowed his breathing and relaxed his shoulders. He listened to the sound of his blood flowing like streams of life under the surface of his skin. He let his head drop forward as his neck relaxed, all the time keeping his eyes on the fog. He willed his arms and legs to relax and he visualized relaxation flowing into his body with every breath of air he took, tension pouring out with every exhalation. He soothed his mind by voiding his thoughts. He opened his soul by giving in to the spirit of the place where he sat, the spirit that manifested as real and tangible at the level of vibrations. He allowed himself to become a commuter train between the vibrations and his awareness.

As usual, nobody was on the train.

"...are your doing, Mr. Jonson?" Bethany's voice pulled Boston back to reality just as he was about to fall asleep. *Some day I'll get it right. Some day.*

"Just getting a feel for the place," he said, shaking his head as he stood up. "Sometimes it helps me to understand the circumstances of the crime a bit more."

Bethany's face froze. Whatever Boston thought he'd seen in her eyes earlier was nothing compared to the smorgasbord he looked into now-flashes of fear, anger, doubt, contempt, vulnerability, hatred. The entire dressed taco with a load on the side. Her mouth opened slowly. And then the words rushed out. "What crime? What crime are you talking about? There was no crime here. It was suicide. He ate himself to death!"

"Maybe," said Boston. "And maybe not."

Bethany glared at him. "The last thing this company needs is a scandal, Mr. Jonson. The instant you make a referral with the word 'crime' in it, the media will crucify Barto Burger."

"I haven't put any words into my referral yet, and I was using the word 'crime' loosely, in the same sense as the scene of the event."

"Then I would prefer you use the word 'event' from now on."

"Provided I don't find evidence of a crime." Boston winked at her. She frowned. He pointed at a door to his left. "Where does that door go?"

Still frowning, Bethany looked in the direction he pointed, thought a moment, and said, "I believe that door would lead to Mr. Barto's sleeping quarters."

"Let's have a look." Boston started toward the door.

"We can't just barge into his bedroom!"

He looked at her. Bethany's eyes were wide, shocked.

"Yes we can, Bethany. It's what I'm here for…to barge into his bedroom and see if there's anything in there that will help me make my referral." He started again to walk toward the door. Bethany sipped from her mug and followed him. Just before they reached the door, she rushed ahead of him and grabbed the door's brass knob. "I hope you realize that anything you see in this room will be…"

"Will be part of my referral if it belongs in it." He looked her in the eye. "Open the door." She sighed loudly, opened the door and stood aside.

Like the checkerboard room, it was sparse-a bed in the center of the floor, just a plain upper mattress and box spring, no headboards or footboards, no posts or canopy. The sheets were white and tucked tight. A wooden desk with a swivel chair faced the wall between two more tall windows with a view of fog. A brass banker's lamp with a dark green shade hovered over a book with a leather cover. Boston walked over to the desk and touched the book. *Yep, genuine leather*. He opened it. There were dates at the top of the page and paragraphs written below.

He kept a diary. Gansheng Barto kept a diary.

He flipped to the last page. June 8. All the pages up to the day of his death-three

weeks of entries - had been torn out. Boston noticed something scribbled along the inside margin.

found a Gantt for pwx, with an updated release date,find out who's doing this

It trailed off into an unintelligible scrawl.

"You'll need a warrant to read that, Mr. Jonson." Bethany reached for the book. She was right. The diary might contain confidential information about the company. He would need a warrant, celebrity CI or not. He let her take it. He'd seen enough anyway. Gansheng Barto started his life with twenty-five years missing, and ended it with three weeks missing.

Chapter 20 - Aftershave

"What do you mean…you don't have…sufficient information…for your referral, Mr. Johnson? The scene has been holographed. The forensics have been gathered. You've spoken to everybody that saw him the day he died. And there are, of course, no signs of foul play. What more do you need?" Mackenzie Beaton stared hard and deadly into Boston's eyes

"I mean I'm not ready to make my referral," said Boston, unphased by the big man's anger, enjoying it. "Something stinks, Beaton." He shrugged his shoulders. "Something just plain stinks, and until I know what it is, I don't make my referral."

They were alone in Beaton's office. Bethany waited in the hall.

It came out slow and quietly controlled, like a sniper taking aim: "I don't know who the hell you think you are, Mr. Jonson. Celebrity or not, I can pull strings in places you never dreamed existed, and cause things to happen, Mr. Jonson." He took one step toward Boston, towering over him, his eyes like two glowing beads of contempt. "Make your referral. Make it quite soon. Make it, and get out of my building."

My building? The boss is gone less than a day, and he's already calling it his building. And how much did he gain when Barto died?

"So this would be a good time to ask you about the new technology?"

"New technology?"

76

"It's supposed to save your company from the wolves. You announced it in an interview. Everybody knows about it, nobody's talking about it. It might help if I know something…"

"That's a matter of extreme secrecy, Mr. Jonson. What could you possibly think that it would have to do with Mr. Barto's suicide?"

"We don't know that it's su…"

"We don't know that it's not."

Boston stepped up quickly, craning his head upward so that his blue nose was almost touching Beaton's nose. "And whether it is or not, and whether you or any of your staff ever decides to cooperate with me or not, all of that will be the focus of my referral. When…I…decide…I'm…ready…to write it." He stepped back. "And you know what?"

Beaton glared a few seconds and grudgingly said, "What?"

"You should think about changing your aftershave. It smells like something an old woman would wear." He winked, and as Beaton's small eyes widened with rage, he spun around and walked out of the office-orange hair flapping on his shoulders-to stir things up in other quarters.

Chapter 21 - Things To Think About While Your Guide Chatters Away On Her Cell Phone

"I'd like to take another look at the Prime Burger," said Boston.

"The Prime? But why? What could it possibly have to do with your referral?" said Bethany peevishly.

"Let's call it inspiration. If it can make a man walk again, maybe it'll help get my referral on its feet."

Fog pushed against the outside panes of the giant windows, giving Boston a sense of chill even though the hall was warm. The air smelled of age as microscopic particulates simulated the decomposition of wood and other materials, an effect created by an architect with a weird sense of realism.

"Maybe you should just make your damned..." Bethany put a finger to her mouth, shushing herself. She breathed deeply and blew the air out loudly. "What I mean, Mr. Jonson, is that if you want to visit the Prime Burger, then that's fine with me. If you really think it will help speed up your referral, then..." All smiles and dimples now. "...then let's go and hang around the Prime until..." She looked down at her robe, reached her hand into a hidden pocket, and pulled out a cell phone. "Yes," she said. She listened a moment and then turned to Boston. "Pardon me for a moment, Mr. Jonson."

Boston nodded as she walked off to the opposite side of the hall with the phone pressed against her ear. She spoke quietly, and then listened. Her face appeared to flare with anger, she spoke again, and then listened.

In the meantime, Boston thought about what he'd learned so far. Gansheng Barto, a vegetarian, had eaten himself to death with hamburgers. Three weeks before his death, he'd changed from bloodless bastard to a happy-go-lucky reformed Scrooge. All the notes in his diary during that perky three weeks were missing. On the page for June 8, right before the missing pages, he'd scrawled in the margin about something called a px, or something. Bethany accidentally let it slip about something, whatever it was, happening again. A man in the Crib who tried to get his attention had mysteriously disappeared. Everyone was tight-lipped and edgy about a new technology. Nobody was leveling with him, nobody was going to cooperate with him, nobody was going to give him dick. He smiled. Things were normal for Boston Jonson, just the way he liked them.

"We're going to show you the new technology, Mr. Jonson."

"Huh?"

"You wanted to know about the new technology. I've just been instructed to take you to our marketing and research planning division and show you the new technology." She pocketed her phone.

"Just like that?"

"Wouldn't want you thinking that we weren't going to cooperate with you, now would we?" She smiled, glanced at her reflection in a pane of glass, and took a sip of coffee.

They walked toward a spot in the wall where, presumably, a door would slide open to reveal an elevator.

Chapter 22 - Non-Disclosure

Blue-robed scribes with quill pens wrote on sheets of brown parchment.

"Tell me that's just for effect," said Boston.

"That's just for effect."

"Really?"

"Really. The parchment is nanopaper, connected to our servers." A dimpled smile. "But the effect is convincing, isn't it?"

Boston nodded, noticing for the first time the absence of inkwells for the pens. "But why?"

"Why what, Mr. Jonson?"

"Why all the medieval décor, the cathedral, the robes? Why make the headquarters for the biggest franchise in the world, using the latest food production technology, into something hundreds of years from the past? Why not just a skyscraper like any other business?"

"Exactly, Mr. Jonson." Bethany sipped some coffee. "We're not just any other business. Besides, it gives our work a kind of flair and solidarity, a sense of belonging and fellowship."

"Like a cult."

Bethany frowned. "No, Mr. Jonson, not like a cult. Our employees are allowed to keep their names."

"So I've heard."

A man in a light brown robe who could have passed for everybody's bald little Friar Tuck approached them. He extended a hand to Boston. "Mr. Jonson, I presume?"

"I've been called worse," said Boston as he grasped the man's hand.

"Larry Peters, head of R&D. We've certainly heard a lot about you, in the e-rags, on NetVision. You're somewhat of a celebrity. Very fortunate to have you referring on Mr. Barto's unfortunate death." He nodded to Bethany. "Ms. Moore."

Boston liked this man. He wondered how long it would take to piss him off. "Thanks, Mr. Peters. One thing...you say you're head of R&D?"

"That's right. For the last five years."

"I thought that was Dr. Toole."

Peters laughed. "You're not the first to make that assumption, Mr. Jonson. Dr. Toole is our chief researcher, one of those who actually does the work of developing new products and enhancing our existing lines. I'm just an administrator. I make sure that Dr. Toole and his staff have everything they need. I take care of business."

"Including the new technology that's supposed to save everybody's asses?"

The flash in Peters' eyes told Boston that it might not take long to piss him off. Bethany slurped loudly from her mug. Boston wondered if it ever ran out of coffee.

"We approve the expenses and handle purchases for the new technology, Mr. Jonson. I've been instructed by Mr. Beaton to discuss it with you, but I hope you realize that I can only give you a high level overview. This technology is..."

"I know. Secret. High level will do."

"Very well then, but first..." He waved to a sheet of paper on a wooden desk; beside it, a ballpoint pen. "We'll need you to sign a non-disclosure agreement."

Boston signed the form and Peters led them through the office as robed figures bent over nano-computers disguised as parchment, quill pens in hand. At the back of the office, a door opened in the stone wall revealing an elevator.

Standing beside Boston in the elevator, Peters said, "That looks to be a nasty injury to your nose, Mr. Jonson. Mind if I ask…"

"Marlee Dunn," said Bethany.

"Oh," said Peters. "Of course."

A few minutes later, they were back in the bowels of The Spit.

Chapter 23 - Where's The Fruit?

It was more like some feudal interrogation cubicle than a conference room: four stone walls, one door, a wooden table and four chairs. A wrinkled woman in a blue robe sat, smiling, in a chair.

"Mr. Jonson," said Peters, "This is Gabby Pinches, our director of new product development."

The old woman peered up at Boston with eyes that sparkled like jewels encased in dried briar. "Gabby Pinches," she said, "Pinch me not." She laughed a long rattling laugh punctuated by a fit of hacking. She pointed at Boston's nose. "Met that Dunn woman, have you?" And she rattled some more.

Boston nodded, smiling sarcastically as he and the other two seated themselves.

"Gabby will tell you about our new technology, which is actually a new product line," said Peters.

"What? That new one?" said Gabby. "That next line of crapola we're gonna shove into their guts?"

"Gabby has a great sense of humor," said Bethany, not smiling.

"Sense of humor, my ass, you little management trollop. I wouldn't eat that stuff if I was starvin' to death on a desert island."

Peters leaned forward. "Gabby…"

"Don't Gabby me, Larry, you fat old ass kisser. I've known you long enough to…"

"…to know that Mr. Barto isn't around to save your ass anymore, Gabby," said Peters. "Better get used to that quickly."

The old woman thought a moment, and then laughed and rattled and hacked. "Don't get me wrong, Jonson. I like to rattle people sometimes." And she rattled some more. "Like to get people goin', you know? Shake things up just fer the helluvit. I think it's all this fog." She waved her hand around to take in the stone windowless walls. "And all this damn stone, is all. Fog an' stone. All I ever see, so busy, you know? So what the hell can I tell you about the new product line?" She leaned toward Peters as though about to speak in confidence, but her voice was loud, brusque. "And which new product line are we talkin' about, Larry?"

Peters lips moved.

"What was that, Larry? The what line?"

"The new burgers." Just barely audible.

"The new burgers? You mean those damn fruit things?"

Peters glared. Bethany glared. Gabby threw her arms up. "Don't know what the big secret is! Fruit burgers! Cloned fruit burgers, Jonson. We got strawberry and peach. Workin' on mango and lemon. Plans in the works for kiwi and blueberry."

"Burgers with fruit in them?" Boston stifled a laugh.

"No, I don't mean burgers with damn fruit in them! Who the hell's gonna buy a damn burger with fruit in it? Any damn fool can open a roll and stuff fruit in, you know?"

"You mean a burger just like the normal Barto burger, with meat, mustard, relish and ketchup, but it tastes like fruit?"

Gabby slapped the table with both hands, emitting a series of guffaws, hacks and rattles. Her body heaved and she slapped the table again. "Now he's got it! Now he's got it! That's the beauty of a cloned burger, don't you see? There's nothing real in it, except what's bred into it. Everything in it is a combination of all the things in it, even the taste! So we can make it taste like anything we want!"

"And you really think they're going to sell?" said Boston.

Bethany sipped from her mug and said, "Picture this, Mr. Jonson-advertisements all over NetVision and on billboards next to schools." She put her hands in front of her as though framing the scene. "Happy faces. Happy children's faces. Happy children with burgers in their hands and their smiling happy lips smeared with blueberry stains even though the real thing won't have any blue in it."

"No great product was ever greater than its marketing," said Peters.

"So I've heard," said Boston. But he knew damned well that this was not the technology to which Beaton had referred in the interview. And he knew these people were trying their damnedest to hide something from him.

Chapter 24 - Jilted

"What do you mean you're not ready to make your referral?" said Bethany. "It never takes this long to make a referral!" Her mouth twisted into something disturbingly close to a snarl. Boston was unphased. He was used to snarls. He counted them when he couldn't sleep.

"It does this time," said Boston.

They were in the main hall. It was noon and people were milling about, a mixture of tourists and robed figures. A crowd of about forty people craned their necks around the Prime Burger as another pretty young guide charmed them with her cooing voice and stories about the Prime. Neutral light filtered through rows of arched windows just as it had in the morning.

"But we've cooperated with you. We've given you everything you've asked for." She pointed downward, vaguely in the direction of the tiny conference room they'd just left. "We even gave you information that you might not have gotten, even with a court order."

"That's right," said Boston.

"Well..." Bethany thought a moment, took a sip from her mug. She frowned and looked into it. Finally. It was empty. Boston was beginning to think that it defied all the laws of matter and energy. "We just wanted to cooperate with you, Mr. Jonson, to expedite your referral. We'd like to see this whole thing taken care of quickly, before our competitors try to use it against us. With Mr. Barto gone, there will be those who think we may be vulnerable, and they may be right."

"I can understand that, Bethany. And I'll make my referral as quickly as I can. But not until I'm ready." As Bethany glared at him, he looked over her shoulder and saw Marlee going into the cafeteria. "I think I'll go for some lunch." Bethany started to walk with him. He turned abruptly toward her. "I'm sure you have things to do, Bethany. I can handle lunch on my own."

Bethany stared at him, puzzled, almost hurt. "But…?"

"I'll meet you back here in about an hour and a half." And he walked toward the door marked CAFETERIA as Bethany stared after him with anything but goodwill in her eyes.

Chapter 25 - Real Food

It wasn't hard to find Marlee. He set his bearings by the sound of a plate smashing on the floor. He found her stooped over, picking up pieces of broken clay, apologizing to a man in a light brown robe.

The cafeteria was a huge stone hall lit by dozens of brass chandeliers with hundreds of robed figures sitting at row upon row of wooden tables with wooden benches, eating silently or talking quietly to those around them. There were none of the usual cafeteria sounds-the steady hum and murmur of voices, clatter and clicks of glasses and plates. This place was dim and subdued, surreal in a spooky way.

Marlee stood up with a handful of broken plate, still apologizing to the back of the brown-robed man when Boston reached her. "You're slipping," he said. "He can still walk."

She gave him a don't-even-think-of-it look and stepped to a waste bin where she let the pieces drop. "I..." she said, "...was watching where I was going. He wasn't."

"OK."

"He wasn't!"

"I believe you."

"Then what's the smile for?

"Just happy to see you."

She rolled her eyes. "Because I'm so charming and beautiful, right?"

"No. Because you're going to buy me lunch."

She cocked her head to the side. "Oh. Right. Lunch. I was thinking about that." She pointed at the line by the food service. "We can wait in line for cloned lunch...or we can go someplace where the food is real." She winked.

"Will I live through it?" Boston winked.

"Depends how hungry you are." She winked again and started walking toward the door.

Boston followed.

Chapter 26 - Rubby In Her Tummy

Boston's nose felt like something dipped in acid and rolled in salt, but that was a small price to pay for Marlee's passionate kisses. She lay beside him with her head snuggled into his chest. "Nothing like a real lunch," said Boston.

A muffled chuckle from Marlee.

"And I lived through it."

A light punch in the stomach. There was a faint smell of something antiseptic in the room, something stronger than the nips of booze he'd seen Marlee swilling back. The bedroom was small but quaint and functional: one bed with canopy and comfortable mattress, one wooden desk with matching chair and reading lamp, one remote-controlled wall-mounted smart screen with SpeedBand CableNet access, one washroom with gravity spa shower, one form-fitting smart bubble chair, one bookcase crowded with genetic engineering textbooks and murder mysteries, including one copy of *Zen and the Art of Investigative Referral* by Boston Jonson (autographed less than an hour ago), one closet with closed door.

But the walls were stone. The ceiling was rib-vaulted. Under the thick gray rug, the floor was rock. And that smell. What was that?

"Does it smell funny in here?" he said.

"Like what?"

"Like a hospital or something. You haven't been drinking rubbing alcohol have you, Marlee Dunn?" he joked.

Marlee lifted her head and glared at him.

"No!" he said, still half-joking.

The glare hardened.

"Rubbing alcohol?" he said. She pushed herself away from him and sat up on the edge of the bed. He propped himself up on his elbow. "That stuff will kill you."

She shrugged her shoulders. "It's just a few sips a day. Enough to keep me sane in this place."

"But rubbing alcohol?"

"Booze is booze. We use it in the labs, so nobody notices it on my breath. Besides, lots of people here drink it."

On the way up to her suite-just before she'd practically raped him-she'd told him that she was a genetic engineer, working in product optimization. She'd been a rising star in the field before coming to Barto Burger, but was now just putting in time, helping a bunch of other science sell-outs find new ways to put fast food into the guts of people who'd forgotten what real food was like.

"It's not booze. It's poison. No wonder you're accident-prone. Do you know what that stuff does to your brain?"

She reached down to her robe on the floor and pulled a metal flask out of a pocket. She opened it and took a small swig. She didn't make a face, but her cheeks flushed. She let out a long breath that almost knocked Boston off the bed. "It keeps me sane, CI guy, and you haven't known me long enough to lecture me. If you want to scold, don't do it in *my* bed."

Boston shrugged. "OK. No lectures. You're a big girl..."

"Right. Big girl. Don't need lectures...need..." She dropped the flask on top of her robe and started to crawl across the bed toward Boston, but the smell of the alcohol was too much. "Sorry Marlee. Can't. That stuff is just..."

She punched him in the ribs and sat up, pouting. "That's what they all say."

Boston smiled. "Maybe you should switch to vodka."

"Lecturing?"

"Maybe I should change the subject." He sat up beside her, serious now. "You know Bethany Moore?"

She frowned. "Yes, unfortunately. Corporate ass-kisser. All wrapped up in herself. She should wear horse blinders with mirrors mounted in them. And I don't think anyone's ever seen her without her coffee mug. She give you the royal tour?"

"Sort of. She mentioned something about something happening, apparently for a second time, and then clammed up. You know of anything happening lately, besides Barto's death, that the company would want to keep quiet?"

"There's a million things this company wants to keep quiet. The whole thing is falling apart. Franchises are going under, class lawsuits are mounting around the planet, supply links to the restaurants are being bought out by the competition and then used against us, and the senior executives are in some kind of war with each other."

"A war? How so?"

"Nobody's sure what it's all about. But the heads of departments used to work together like a well-oiled machine, weekly meetings of senior managers, you'd see them walking through the halls or sitting in the cafeteria talking shop. But now, you never see them together. They stick to their offices. And it got worse a few weeks ago when Barto started getting a bad case of the smilies. That was scary."

"Why scary?"

"Because he used to be such an unsmiling bastard. But he was in charge. It gave everybody a sense of security knowing that the man running things was really running things and that no matter how bad they were, if anybody could bring us through it, he could. And then he was suddenly walking around shaking everybody's hand, giving people the day off, giving entire departments the day off, but the scary part was watching the managers and executives. They were starting to look worried. There were a lot of whispered phone calls. Weird."

Boston thought about this and said, "Did anything happen similar to what happened to Barto?"

"You mean a suicide?"

"I don't know. Maybe somebody eating himself to death?"

Marlee chuckled. Boston noticed that it made her cheeks round and red, and her mouth twisted in a devil-may-care way. She looked at Boston and saw that he wasn't smiling. She considered for a moment and said, "You know, there was something a few months ago." She sat up straight. "Rogers. One of the researchers in product development."

"You mean Carl Rogers, the one in the news? They kept his body and stuck it in the catacombs?"

"Right. They're at the bottom-most level of the building. Deep underground. I've never seen them, but I've heard they're like something out of the Middle Ages."

Boston looked around the room. "You've gotta be joking. The Middle Ages?"

Marlee laughed, cheeks flushing. "Not exactly like the rest of the building. The rest is a copy. The stone is molded smart material. Try putting a rock through any of the stained glass windows. You'd need a uranium-tipped shell to put a dent in them. But the vaults in the catacombs were imported. All the stone is real, and I've heard that some of the walls are carved right out of the rock foundation." She bent forward, excitement in her voice. "And that whole thing with Carl Rogers was really weird. *He* was really weird."

"How so?" said Boston, leaning forward.

"He kept to himself even though he was one of the top managers and should have been schmoozing constantly and been surrounded by ass-kissers all the time. But he never talked to anybody and you'd never see him in the cafeteria. But then, all the people in the area he worked in were sort of like that I guess, secretive. Bunch of unsociable weirdoes. They used to work into the night and right on through weekends."

"And working long hours is unusual?"

"No, not really. But they were just weird about it, like they were cut off from the rest of the world. Nobody was ever allowed into their sector. And Carl, well, he was even weirder than the others. Nervous and bug-eyed and nothing like a manager. Just work, work, work. That's what they were all like. Always working. And they never spoke to anybody from any of the other departments. If you said hello, they just ignored you. Whatever the work was, it took them over completely. But when Carl died, everything changed."

"Changed?"

"Yeah. Well, to begin with, Carl was alive one day, dead the next."

"Well, Marlee, that's what happens when people die."

'No, it wasn't just like he'd died. It was all so strange. Nobody saw him die. We heard that it was a heart attack but, it was like, he just disappeared. One day he was walking through the halls solving problems in his head, the next he was buried in the catacombs and not even his family was allowed to see him. But the weirdest part…" She pushed herself up and pivoted around on her rump so that she was sitting upright and facing Boston. She put a hand on his arm. "The weirdest part was that they closed the entire sector he was working in. All the others were shipped out to other parts of the world. It was like that whole product development section never even existed."

"Because one person had a heart attack?"

Marlee smiled widely and bounced on the bed. "That's what I mean! The whole thing was weird. They closed a multimillion-dollar product research department with some of the most expensive scientists in the world working in it, over what? Somebody dying from natural causes."

"If they were natural causes."

Marlee bounced again. "They weren't, were they? He didn't die from a heart attack, did he?"

"I don't know. But it sounds strange. And that could explain why Bethany would suddenly clam up. She said she'd get back to me about it."

Marlee laughed. "And you really believe that?"

"No. She'll cook up a story."

"There's a lot of that around here."

"I noticed. I talked to a woman named Gabby Pinches today."

"Gabby? I know her."

"She knows you."

"Knew right away it was me that did in your nose, didn't she?"

"You got it."

"Yeah, well, she's great anyway. She doesn't take shit from anybody. And she's one of the most brilliant scientists in the company, believe it or not, and one of the senior people who seems to be in the middle of the management war."

"Good guy or bad guy."

"Good. Definitely good."

"I had a feeling she was holding out."

"There's strange things going on in here, lover boy, people are hunkering down and covering their asses."

Boston shrugged. "I guess so." He thought for a moment. "Think she's senior enough to get me into the catacombs for a look at Carl Rogers' body…without Beaton or anyone else knowing about it?"

Marlee bounced off the bed with a flash of pink nipples and jet black bush that almost sucked the irises out of Boston's head. "I'm coming too!" she yelled. "I'll talk to Gabby. She'll do it for me. She likes me. She thinks I'm…different. She'll do it for me."

Boston gawked, feeling the tug on his irises. *Different. Oh yes, different.*

Marlee clapped her hands gleefully. "We're going into the catacombs!"

Catacombs. Boston felt the chill that had crept across his skin earlier.

Chapter 27 - Confessional

"Do you think he suspects?"

"He's an idiot."

"But…his reputation…"

"He's a fool."

She huddled in a wooden chair in a small candle lit room dominated by a towering wooden structure decorated with intricate carvings of paisley-like patterns and a door made of two quilts with obscure patterns that resembled animals and people but, up close, were just meaningless patterns.

She peered into a black mesh screen in the structure. "He asks pointed questions."

"He's just trying to throw you off," said a deep raspy voice.

"I hate him," she said.

"There's nothing wrong with hating him as long as you cooperate with him and don't give him anything."

"But what about Kemper? He tried to signal him. I saw him do it. Kemper knows everything."

"Not any more. We've taken care of Kemper. You take care of Jonson. Take care of him by using your brains and not panicking."

"Yes. You're right. Keep cool. Take care of him." She thought a moment. "Should I fuck him?"

"No, don't fuck him. Just play along with him."

"Right." She sipped from her coffee cup and sat, alone now with her thoughts. How to get rid of Boston Jonson without raising suspicion. Couldn't be too hard…if he were an idiot and a fool.

But why can't I fuck him?

Chapter 28 - Ruthless People Who Exploit Old Ladies

Boston and Marlee and had just left Marlee's apartment when Boston's wallet buzzed him. He took it out and flipped it open. A woman's head appeared in the tiny monitor. "Been another death at The Spit, Boston."

"When?"

"Just reported."

"Details?"

"Male. Caucasian. Mid-thirties. Name of Luke Kemper."

"Oh no!" piped Marlee. "I know him!"

"Who's that?" said the woman in the monitor.

"Where's the body?" said Boston.

"Someone will meet you at the main reception. Who's voice was that?"

"None of your business."

"Your referral on the Barto death is slow." The woman craned her head around as though she were trying to see beyond the boundaries of the monitor. "Any problems, Boston? Distractions? Anything we should know about?" The woman winked.

"No, Laurel. Things are under control."

"We have the body on ice and the holos on file. But we can't do anything with them until we get the referral."

"I know, Laurel, and the referral will be done soon. Just need a few more details. And this new death is probably connected."

"What are you on to, Boston?"

"Don't know yet, Laurel. Bye."

"Wait…"

Boston folded his wallet and slipped it into his pocket. He turned to Marlee. "What do you know about Kemper?"

"I worked with him on a few projects. Cloned sauces, mustard profiling. You know, the usual stuff. And then he was put on something really hush-hush in the deep levels."

"The deep levels?"

"Where the really secret stuff is-early stages of new products, when the competition can do the most damage if they get on to it, strategic product development, like long-term products that they haven't even started to develop, but they kick around and figure out if the market research and other projected products make them viable. They also do product enhancement there. That's the most secret of all for some reason. Nobody knows what happens in that area except the people who work it-and that's what Luke was working in, at least…"

"Yes?"

"…until a few weeks ago. Suddenly, he was out of the lower levels and working in the Crib. That's like a demotion or something. We used to talk and have lunch together, but after he left product enhancement, he became really antisocial, stopped talking to everybody, ate by himself, never showed up at any of the social areas. And he used to be really friendly. Had a bad habit of chewing toothpicks though."

"What was that? He chewed toothpicks?"

"Yeah, all the time. They stuck out of his mouth like you see farmers in pictures with bits of straw dangling out of their mouths. Why? What's that got to do with...?"

"And he was suddenly put out of a top secret area a few weeks ago? Was it three weeks? Four weeks? Two weeks?"

Marlee thought a moment. "I saw him in the Crib for the first time...let me see, yeah, almost exactly three weeks ago. Why?"

"I'm not sure." Boston wrapped one arm across his chest and rested the elbow of his other arm on it. He punched his chin lightly with the side of his index finger a few times while he thought. Then his face lightened and he gently grabbed both of Marlee's arms. "You line up a tour of the catacombs with Gabby. I have to examine Kemper's body. I have a feeling there's more than suicides and fruit burgers going around here. Be careful. Call me in a couple of hours at bjonson."

"And you be careful too," said Marlee. "Remember, the people who run this place aren't just powerful, they're ruthless." She thrust her head forward and planted a quick kiss on Boston's lips. "They exploit old ladies."

Boston didn't know whether to smile or frown, so he left.

What's this body going to look like? he thought as he walked to a section of wall that he hoped would open to reveal an elevator.

It did.

Chapter 29 - Somehow A Murder

"I suppose, of course, this means that you'll be around here...a while longer, Mr. Jonson?" The tone in Beaton's words was clear: When the hell are we going to get rid of you?

"I'm sure the prospect of having me around a while longer warms your heart, Beaton." Beaton's eyes narrowed. They were in a men's washroom, a long narrow feudal men's washroom with stone walls and no windows. Wooden beams bracketed the low ceiling. Ten doorless stalls lined one wall. Boston peered into one of them and gagged back the laughter. The stall contained a large porcelain bowl and a metal support rod about chest high over the bowl. "Can't afford indoor plumbing?"

Beaton glared. "The bowls are equipped with lasers that keep them cleaner than most drinking fountains." He stopped short, frowned. "We like to maintain the building's atmosphere as much as possible." He pointed to the end of the long room where two men in dark brown robes hovered around the last stall. "No one, of course, has touched anything."

"You're learning, Beaton," said Boston as he walked past the big man. "You're learning."

Beaton stared coldly as Boston ambled up to the men at the end of the room. He noticed a trace of cinnamon in the air. He looked around, but other than the stalls and the washstands opposite them, there were no air fresheners. *Must be mini-jets in the ceiling. Nice touch.* The two men stepped aside like petals opening on a terrible flower. One of them pointed into the stall.

Slouched against the big white bowl, his hood down and the front of his blue robe soaked with blood, the body of Luke Kemper lay lifeless, his face frozen into a soundless scream. Bloody toothpicks spilled from his mouth. His white hands clutched bundles of them. Open boxes of toothpicks were strewn on the floor around Kemper's body. Boston was certain now. This was the man who had tried to get his attention in the Crib. This man had wanted to talk to Boston, but he'd been too afraid to approach him. And then he'd disappeared. And now he was dead. And it looked like suicide, like he'd eaten toothpicks until they'd torn the life out of his insides. Blood still oozed from his mouth.

It was time to ride the vibration super highway.

Boston closed his eyes. He breathed deeply, slowly. He exhaled slowly, emptying every molecule of air from his lungs and then forcing more. He breathed in again and let his mind wander aimlessly, refusing to attach itself to any details or emotions, just wandering without purpose in the energy fields that define existence. He allowed his mind to seep into those fields and flow with their current. He allowed his mind to sink into the current and fall effortlessly through atoms and neutrons and into the most basic stuff of the universe: vibrations. He opened his soul to their message and heard something. It started as a faraway rumble and grew into a churning spasm that seemed to center in the area of his stomach. Just when he thought he could discern its cosmic message, he realized that he was listening to the sound of his stomach growling.

It looked like Marlee's *real* lunch wasn't going to keep his engine running. *Better than what this poor sucker ate, though*, he thought, gazing at Kemper's slouched body. He turned toward Beaton but he was gone. He looked at one of the robed men and said, "The big guy not like the sight of blood?" The man did not answer. He stood motionless. "Right."

Boston walked toward the door.

Suicide my ass. Somehow, this is murder.

Chapter 30 - Hurt

Boston stood by the men's room door talking into his wallet. His wallet talked back. "Why are you taking so long on this, Boston?" asked Laurel. "Everything's in. If you suspect something's wrong, refer it to an investigative body. You're getting dangerously outside your mandate on this one and people are starting to get pissed off."

"Like I've never pissed anyone off before," said Boston.

"These people can hurt you."

Boston thought a moment. Laurel was right. Even a celebrity CI such as himself could be surfing the job sites in short order if his bosses had a hot enough political fire burning under their asses, and MacKenzie Beaton had the power to stoke him into the cold. But he hadn't turned up the heat that much yet, and Boston wondered about that. He hadn't been outright ordered to lay off. Beaton was holding back for the time being. He was pissed, but why hadn't he just had Boston taken right off the referral and replaced by someone more cooperative? A move like that would obviously attract some attention, ruffle a few feathers among the other CIs, and provoke a few questions-maybe even from the media-but the whole thing would peter out and Barto's death would be old news in a week or two. Beaton was holding back.

It was time for Boston to turn up his own heat.

"And maybe I can hurt them," he said wistfully.

"What?"

"Oh nothing. Better send a crew over for the body."

"And your referral?"

"Soon."

"How soon?"

"As soon as I'm ready." He saw Bethany heading toward him, coffee mug in hand, all smiles and dimples.

"Gotta go now."

"But…?"

He snapped his wallet shut.

Chapter 31 - Where's the Note?

"I just heard," said Bethany. Steam curled over the top of her cup. Boston wondered how much mileage she would get on the refill. *Probably the rest of the afternoon.* "Do you know who it was?"

"Luke Kemper."

Bethany cocked her head slightly and pursed her lips as though trying to remember something. "I don't think I know him."

"Then why was he afraid of you in the Crib?" said Boston.

"I beg your pardon?"

"Nothing. Did you find out what it was that 'happened again'?"

"What happened again?"

"You tell me. You let it slip this morning."

"Let it *slip*?" Her face turned red. She glared at him.

A lot of glaring in this place. Good.

"I don't know what kind of game you're playing, Mr. Jonson, but…"

"He ate himself to death with toothpicks."

Bethany stepped back. "Toothpicks?" she whispered.

"Small slivers of wood used to…"

"I know what they are, Mr. Jonson, but I'm having difficulty understanding what you're saying. No one can eat himself to death on toothpicks."

"Kemper did." Boston pointed toward the men's room door. "He's lying in there in a small lake of blood from…"

"How will this affect your referral?" Her eyes were cold, calculating.

"It means that now I have two referrals to make, and it looks like they're connected."

"Connected? How can you...?"

"Two suicides, Bethany. Two. They both ate themselves to death."

"But..."

"On hamburgers and toothpicks. In less than a day of each other. I'd say they're connected, and I'd say they both look suspicious. Wouldn't you?" It was his turn to glare at her.

Bethany thought a moment. "Maybe it's some kind of bug."

Boston scowled. Bethany blushed.

"*I* don't know," she said quickly. "Nothing like *this* has ever happened before." She seemed to be looking past Boston. He followed her gaze to a brass light fixture on the wall, highly polished and reflective. "But what could be suspicious about suicide? Lately, this company has been the target of scandals, corporate espionage, legal suits-you name it. It's put a tremendous amount of pressure on our employees. It's not unusual for people to take their own lives when the stress becomes too great for them."

"From what I've heard, Mr. Barto was anything but stressed. He seemed to have been in better spirits before his death than at any time in his life. Kemper was demoted recently. That might have..."

"How did you know..." Suddenly suspicious. A light thread of steam coiled into the air over her

110

cup. "I mean, what makes you think that? That he was demoted?"

Boston ignored the question. "But to eat himself to death with toothpicks? In a men's room? No way. Nobody does that. Guns, poison, jumping off buildings, but not toothpicks. And not hamburgers. And both of them are missing the main ingredient in a suicide."

"What's that?"

"The note. Neither of them left a note. I find that very suspicious."

Bethany tweaked her eyebrows and thought for a moment. "So what do you think it is? If it's not suicide, then what?"

"I don't know yet, but there's something going on here. You said you didn't know Kemper. Is there any reason he should be afraid of you?"

"Of course not! I didn't even know him. Why would he be afraid of me? And why do *you* think he was afraid of me?"

"He was in the Crib this morning. He was going to approach me, but you turned toward him and he backed off. Just before we talked to Toole, he disappeared. Now he's dead. Do you have any idea why he might be dead?"

"No!" Her eyes narrowed viciously. "I told you, I didn't know him. And if he didn't approach you this morning then it had nothing to do with me. Or maybe that was something you just imagined!"

She backed away from him and he could see that she was forcing her breath under control, calming herself. She glanced at herself in the brass lights, sipped from her mug, and her face relaxed.

She was good. Maybe too good. "What do you want to do now?" she said in an even voice, as though nothing had happened.

Boston considered: he wasn't going to get anything useful from her, Toole, or Beaton. If he pushed them any further at this point, he would just be pulling the shit release valve on himself. It was time to back off, at least until he had some more ammunition, something concrete that he could throw into their glaring faces. He didn't want to get tossed off this referral yet. No, not until he'd had a chance to find out a little more about Barto, and those missing three weeks.

"Let's go back to the Prime," he said.

Bethany looked puzzled, but nodded. "If you want to, Mr. Jonson."

"Boston."

112

Chapter 32 - The Stuff of Legend and Myth

The Main Hall, as usual, was cavernous and crowded. Tourists in sweaters and cameras, and employees in robes and hoods milled about like sand in a whirling wind. At the center of it all, silent and imperious, the Prime Burger, parent to trillions, reigned in its pyramid case. Boston and Bethany stood before it. Bethany sipped from her mug, bored. Neither the brushed stone base nor the slanting surface of the crystal case offered her a mirror. The Prime hogged it all. She would just have to guess how she looked. Boston stared at the Prime Burger. He thought it looked small for something that had spawned a global empire. It was the same size as any of its legion of offspring. It looked the same and, presumably, it smelled and tasted the same. Take it out of the case and put it in a Barto Burger restaurant and it would be lost in its own conformity.

Yet it was the stuff of legend and myth. It had the power to awe, the power to make a crippled man throw down his crutches and walk again. It was the symbol of a corporate entity that could draw normal human beings into its ranks where they would willingly lose their identities in the depths of hoods and robes. Though, they could keep their names. This entire hall was designed to inspire wonder and a sense of otherworldly majesty emanating directly from the area where the Prime was displayed like a royal presence or a religious relic.

"This is one helluva weird place," said Boston.

Bethany looked at him, blank-faced.

Getting used to me, he thought.

"I suppose you would be an expert on that subject, Mr. Jonson," she said.

"Good one, Bethany. I think we may actually get along."

"Whatever you say." She looked back at the Prime. "And what exactly are we here for? Do you suspect the Prime of something?"

"No. Just hoping for a little inspiration, maybe a little understanding of this place." He stared at the Prime for a moment more and turned to Bethany. "Have you noticed any strange behavior in the senior managers lately?"

"What kind of strange behavior?"

"Oh, just about anything out of the normal, I suppose. Notice any hostility, lack of cooperation, arguments, gunfights?"

"Gun…?"

"Just joking. About the gunfights. But not about the rest." He turned his whole body to face her. "I know that Mr. Barto was in great spirits for the last few weeks. That was apparently out of character. Have you noticed any other senior people acting out of character?"

Bethany thought a moment, shrugged. "No."

"No feuding or infighting?"

She sighed loudly. "What exactly do you want me to say, Mr. Jonson? I told you that I haven't noticed any unusual behavior. Only in Mr. Barto.

But he obviously wasn't as good humored as he seemed or he wouldn't have killed himself."

"*If* he killed himself."

"And if he didn't?"

"I don't know."

"Then, why don't you just write your referral to the agency that can find out? I thought that was supposed to be your job."

"It was."

"Was?"

"I'll write it when I'm ready. But I'm not ready yet. I have questions."

"Then ask them and I'll get you the answers."

"OK. Let's assume we have two cases of suicide."

Bethany's face beamed with smiles and dimples.

"I mean, the stress from bad publicity, legal suits, competition...all the things you mentioned have been so terrible that Mr. Barto cracked, all happy on the surface and self-destructive deep inside, and Kemper...well, he just broke up and ate himself to death on toothpicks. Does that seem like a reasonable scenario?"

"Yes, Mr. Jonson. It's what I've been saying all along. The pressure on us has been a nightmare. And like you said, it's affected the senior management, made most of us edgier than normal. Things just aren't the way they used to be, the way they should be." She sipped from her mug. "I really do think that you should refer the whole thing to a mental health unit."

"Can you think of anyone who would want to kill Mr. Barto?"

Chapter 33 - Oops, Again

"You may think that you can hide behind your celebrity, Mr. Jonson." Beaton's voice was disturbingly calm. "But I've learned a few things about you. I've talked to people in government, high up, of course, in government. I've talked to people in agencies. High up in agencies."

"Of course," said Boston, smirking.

Beaton ignored him. "You're vulnerable, Mr. Jonson. Quite vulnerable." A tiny malicious smile formed drifted across Beaton's fish mouth.. "You may have established a reputation for making brilliant referrals, but you've also made many enemies. You've alienated people in all the organizations for whom you've worked: the police, hospitals, and mental health agencies, just to name a few. Your reputation is built just as much on insults and insubordination as it is on your referral abilities."

"As I recall, you specifically requested me for this referral."

"Something I'm beginning to regret."

"I have that effect on people."

"You might want to be careful of the effect you have on people here, Mr. Jonson."

"Is there a reason for telling me all this?"

The smile dropped from Beaton's lips. He stared and breathed a moment, expressionless, lips quivering. He said, "Yes, of course, Mr. Jonson, there is." He paused, a hint of the malicious smile peeking out from the edges of his mouth. "You have until tomorrow morning to wrap up the referrals for both Mr. Barto and Mr. Kemper, or you will be replaced by a new CI. And if you refer for anything other than suicide, then, of course, you will never make another referral again."

"You can't..."

"Yes, I can. And I did. And you have until tomorrow morning. Now, get out of my office."

Oops, thought Boston. *Time to speed things up.*

And then a strange thought crossed his mind: Why was Beaton giving him until the next day?

Chapter 34 - Three Questions

"Squealer."

Bethany's jaw all but dove into her mug. She stood, mug to chin, the sip she was about to take frozen in mid flow. Boston loved having this effect on people. But it lasted only a few seconds. She half-scowled, gave up on sipping and said, "I don't think you're in any position to know anything about my sex life, Mr. Jonson."

"What are you talking about?"

"How would you know that I...?" If the color red were heat, Bethany's head would have been in flames. "I mean..."

It was too cruel. He had to rescuer her. "You told Beaton that I asked if you knew who might want to kill Mr. Barto."

"I..." Her lips pursed, she glanced from side to side, trapped with no mirror is sight. Seeing no way out, she became the cornered rat. She attacked. "Unlike you, I report to *my* boss in a timely manner."

And after he'd just been merciful. "Unlike you, I get the facts before I report."

A baleful look. "Unlike..."

"Oh, let's just drop it. You want me out of here so that you can cover up whatever it is you want to cover up so that your little burger empire won't get smeared in the media." He swung around, orange hair flying out, and pushed his face within an inch of hers. "Tell you what." He put a forefinger on her chin. "Answer three questions for me and I'll make my referral and get out of your hair, and you can cover up whatever you want, no questions from me. Ever again. Deal?"

"What three questions?"

"Haven't got a clue. I'll get back to you on that."

He spun away from her and started to walk down the hall.

"Where are you going?" Bethany called after him.

"We need to talk to Toole again," he said without looking back. *And I need Marlee to get me into those catacombs ASAP*.

Chapter 35 - A Really Cool Rock Concert Lighted Place

Jimi Hendrix towered above Boston, grinding impossible sounds out of his VooDoo Stratocaster as Janis Joplin howled the blues on the cover of Big Brother. There was something fitting about dead rock stars in Dr. John Jonathan Toole's living quarters with their high stone walls and ponderous wooden doors. Oversized posters slapped haphazardly at weird angles, some overlapping others, covered most of the stone. Giant black lights far up on the ceiling cast a cool blue glow over the shelves constructed of wooden planks, red bricks, and concrete building blocks that lined the book-packed walls. The books were in no apparent order- *Mutants: On Genetic Variety and the Human Body* was squashed between the *Whole Earth Catalog* and *Danger in the Valleys of Mars.*

Toole lay back on a plastic nano-bubble couch, its surface seeming to breathe as it massaged his back and legs. He was smiling.

"Hey man," he said. "That was really effed up down in the Crib. (blink, blink) I mean, like, maybe sometimes I get a little sensitive about the Dr. John thing, but I'm willing to call it just, you know, like something under the bridge." He tapped his jaw nervously a few times with the side of his right index finger. "I get that a lot, but I guess you were just pushing...like Sam Spade or Travis Macgee."

Boston noticed titles from Dashiel Hammett and Nero Wolfe among the books piled on the wooden planks. Small round silver objects studding all four walls from top to bottom-a 360 wireless nanopod fully integrated surround sound system. Toole took his music seriously.

"You got it, Doctor," said Boston. "Never could stand a blank piece of paper, or a pool of water without ripples."

Toole slapped his knee. "I knew it! I knew it! You, like, really are the genius they say you are. Effin' A!"

"And I appreciate you letting me talk to you in your private quarters, Doctor."

Bethany stood uneasily beside Boston-there were no reflective surfaces in the room. "Yes," she said cautiously. "This is very generous of you, Doctor Toole." She seemed almost suspicious.

Toole beamed, eyes wide and round behind the globe lenses of his spectacles. With all the technology in the walls of this room alone, Boston wondered why he didn't just get his eyes nano-enhanced, but then, looking at the 60s rock posters, he guessed the glasses were more for effect…probably not even prescription.

"I don't entertain often," said Toole. "I like my solitude, just like Gansheng did. I like to travel back to the 60s. They were exciting times. The music is almost mystical and speaks of optimism and hope."

Boston noticed the abrupt change in the way Toole spoke, like somebody several degrees separated from effin' A.

"Hey," said Boston, pointing to one of the posters. "Dark Side of the Moon...best Rock n' Roll album of all time."

"Effin' A, man!" The other Toole was back. "The lunatics are in the garden! And Money rocks like nothin' else. The sax solo is, like, the most expansive wall of sound since...well (blink, blink)...All Along the Watchtower."

Boston pointed to a ten foot high reproduction of the cover of Morrison Hotel. "Road House Blues," he said. "Best rock single ever."

Toole threw his arms up. "Effin' ever!"

"You've got great taste in music, Doctor," said Boston, scanning the album covers of bands that most people had forgotten. "Velvet Underground, Electric Prunes, Steppenwolf...you've got 'em all."

Toole beamed so brightly, it was almost loud. He motioned toward two more bubble chairs. "Sit down, sit down. Let's talk."

Boston got right into it. "I know I'm being a pain in the ass." He glanced quickly at Bethany and then back to Toole. "But I've never had a referral like this before, and-as everyone has been making clear to me-this one needs to be handled with discretion."

Bethany nodded agreement.

Toole frowned.

Boston continued, "I want to get out of here just as much as everybody else wants me to get out of here. But..." He suddenly felt completely relaxed the moment his butt settled in the chair. Nothing like a little nano massage while he stirred up shit with the good doctor.

"Cool chair," he said. "Have to get one of these for those rare moments when I'm home. But back to business, I want to wrap this up as quickly as possible so that I can spend some of those rare moments at home, and get out of everybody's hair." He glanced at Bethany and noticed that she seemed relieved in spite of not being able to monitor her looks every ten seconds. "You were closer to Mr. Barto than anyone else. If he killed himself, then I can make a psych referral and get a team of psychologists in for remedial counseling and follow-up consequence services. But I have to tie up a few loose ends … you know…a second death…Kemper…kind of similar circumstances to Mr. Barto's death. Both suicides. Or so I'm told to believe, but no suicide notes. And, uh, I'd say the suicides are just a little bizarre, wouldn't you?"

The nanos in Bethany's chair must have been working double time. Her eyes were wide and her body was about as erect as the human form could muster in a reclining position. She was about to speak when Toole preempted her.

"Gansheng was the only friend I ever had," he said, sounding more like the stranger who'd popped out a few minutes earlier. "He was a cold, calculating bastard who derived great joy from exploiting people. To him, people were mechanisms that you programmed to do what you wanted, and it didn't ever matter what they wanted-they were just parts of a huge money-making machine."

"But he seems to have had a change of heart…"

124

"Maybe on the surface..." He shut up abruptly, glanced at Bethany and then back to Boston. "In his last few weeks..." And Boston knew that another layer of crap was about to be slopped over the truth. Toole paused for a few seconds and continued, "I couldn't believe it. Nobody could. It was completely against everything he ever stood for. He started treating people like...people, like things with hearts and souls. He smiled all the time. I caught him humming to himself once. Gansheng was never a hummer, at least, not the Gansheng who built Barto Burgers on the backs of old ladies and people who gladly poisoned their bodies on cloned junk food."

"And you have no idea what happened? No idea what could have caused such a dramatic change of heart?"

"It was right out of the blue. Like he went to bed one person and woke somebody else."

"And just how close were the two of you?" Toole's eyes squinted momentarily and he seemed to tense up. "I mean, did you spend a lot of time together?"

Toole thought about this for a moment and then loosened up. "Naw," he said. "We're both loners. I have my music and work, and Barto had his world domination, and that was taking up more time with all the problems we've been having, especially our cloning process getting to our competitors. We expected that to happen sooner or later, but not nearly this soon. When he wasn't in meetings or on the road, he was in his quarters upstairs just, thinking."

125

"Thinking?"

"If you'd seen his quarters, you'd know. He has a balcony that nobody can reach and a bunch of weird statues, and a chair in the middle of his living room. No other furniture. Just an old chair. He sat in it for hours staring out the window at the fog. He loved the fog. I think that's why he built the headquarters here, for the fog."

Bethany leaned forward and began to speak, "I don't think you need to..."

"I saw his rooms," said Boston. "Sparse."

"Like his soul," said Toole. "Until a few weeks ago."

"And there was nothing to suggest that he might be having a change of heart before then...in the least out of character?"

"Well," said Toole. "He quashed a major project we had on the go, but that was more likely because of the legal..."

"I think we can leave Mr. Barto's business decisions out of this," said Bethany, glaring angrily. "I don't think they would have any bearing on his personal life or on his suicide."

"So it *was* suicide?" said Toole, glancing from Boston to Bethany and back.

"Haven't ruled it out," said Boston. He wasn't sure if the look that Bethany shot at him was anger, relief or worry. Everything about her seemed to be out of kilter when she had nothing around that would allow her to see herself. "Tied in with Kemper's death-and the way they both died-it seems unusual, but..."

126

The sparkle was back in Toole's eyes. (blink, blink) "You must've seen a lotta effin' weird stuff in your referrals, man. I remember reading about the Time Lock Incident. Man! Did you really travel back in time on that one?"

"According to the media, I did," said Boston.

"And what about according to Boston Jonson?"

"I honestly don't think his opinion matters anymore."

"It does here," said Toole.

"OK," said Boston. "I traveled in time. But not back."

"You mean you went forward?

"Nope."

"Then..."

"I traveled to the present."

Toole and Bethany stared at Boston blank-faced. Boston noticed a pile of books in a corner of the room. Unlike the others, they were book-marked and some were open against the floor, as though they were in recent use. He noticed the words Praeder-Willi in some of their titles. Just as Toole was breaking out of his trance, Boston asked, "What's Praeder-Willi?"

Bethany looked about ready to shit her pants.

Chapter 36 - The Praeder-Willi Rock

"It was an effin' dead end," said Toole. "Seemed great at first, but it fizzled out the closer we looked at it and then it just, like, effin' died on us."

There was something oddly funny about Bethany's frozen posture in a form-fitting nano-enhanced chair, something almost ugly in the mismatch, if not bizarre. Boston loved the effect. "What was the dead end?" he asked, as he glanced quickly at Bethany to see the effect. A wince. *Yes!*

"Effin' people and their diets, man," said Toole. "We couldn't get 'em to buy into the no fat, no calorie, no cholesterol, no toxins, no anything that could possibly hurt an effin' fly, and probably make them live to a hundred and, like, fifty. It was the perfect food! But they didn't effin' want it. It was too good to be true. They figured it would have to taste different. Not bad, just different. Not like a burger. People were already having a hard time swallowing the concept of a one-piece cloned burger." He grinned at his pun. Boston smiled. Bethany sat frozen. Toole continued. "I'll keep this as simple as possible. Praeder-Willi syndrome is a genetic eating disorder. We were studying Praeder and other disorders hoping to come up with a burger that would turn the appetite off for the rest of the evening after eating it. That way people wouldn't overeat in the evening. But the whole thing was just too effed up. There were moral and legal implications, and the science wasn't going to work, at least, not in our lifetimes."

"So it was scrapped," said Boston.

"Effin' right," said Toole. "Twenty-five mil in research down the effin' toilet. Scrapped PWX and all the associated studies a year ago."

PWX. The pwx mentioned in Barto's journal. But according to the journal, Barto was looking into a Gantt chart he'd found with an updated release. He decided to keep this to himself for the time being.

"We're fast food," said Toole. "Always gonna turn away the health food crowd for the fat food crowd." He looked around at the posters on his walls. "But there's bigger things than effin' food."

"Born To Be Wild," said Boston, pointing to a life-size photo of Steppenwolf gyrating under red and blue lights. "Nastiest rock single on the freeway."

"Effin' A, man!" Toole grabbed a remote from a paisley plastic table beside his chair and touched in three numbers. Guitar music blasted out of the tiny nano speakers in the walls and John Kay's voice boomed through the room...GET YOUR MOTOR RUNNIN'...HEAD OUT ON THE HIGHWAY...LOOKIN' FOR ADVENTURE...

The room went dark and suddenly exploded with psychedelic lights as Toole sprang up and began air banding the song, banging an invisible guitar.

Strange, thought Boston, *the bios said he wanted to be the drummer. And why does he still have all those books out a year later?* He looked at

129

Bethany. She was standing, her eyes wavering between anger and horror. It was time to leave.

130

Chapter 37 - An Infinite Number of Angry Bethanys

The smell of malice hung in the elevator like strange food. Bethany observed her anger in the thousands of reflections of elevator mirror, pure rage repeating itself into endless horizons and not the largest or the smallest or multiplication of her image into eternity was enough to cool her mood. Topping it off, her cup was empty.

"I hope you realize that everything that was said in that room was confidential, Mr. Jonson," she said.

"Boston."

She motioned to take a drink, looked into the cup and clucked her tongue. "And not just everything he said...his behavior as well. Dr. Toole is one of the most brilliant minds in the world. If anything like his little outburst were to make it into the media, he would be a laughingstock. And that would reflect on Barto Burgers. We've already had flack over this thoughts on cloning rock..."

"Dr. Toole's love for sixties music won't be in my referral."

Bethany's shoulders relaxed and her mood loosened.

"He sure does do a mean air guitar, though, doesn't he?"

In the elevator mirrors, an infinite number of Bethanys stabbed Boston Jonson to death with their deadly glares.

Chapter 38 - Old Rubby Buddies

"That's priceless!" screamed Marlee. "And she just walked away and left you in the main hall? Just left you there?"

They were back between the cozy stone walls of Marlee's bedroom, and they had a visitor, someone who claimed to have interesting information, and so far the information had been *very* interesting. Beth Petersen was a cute little brunette with a beautifully dimpled smile, big brown eyes, and the perkiest breasts since frozen Jello. She and Marlee were sharing a flask of rubbing alcohol they poured into cups with lime Gatorade.

"Nobody's *ever* bumped her can that hard," squealed Beth. Her voice was crisp, but soothing; her laugh deep and throaty, and there was something in her demeanor, a quiet sensuality that spoke of expensive Victoria Secrets under her blue robe, prompting more than one dirty little thought in Boston's head, alone in Marlee's bedroom with two rubbied beauties. *Bad Boston*, he thought. *Get your mind out of there*.

"Now, let's not be too critical of the poor woman," said Boston. They looked at him dropped-jawed. "She'd just come from a place with no reflective objects into a small box with mirrored walls. I think she'd just experienced an uncontrollable check-myself-out surge."

They howled.

"And she was out of coffee." They howled louder. Marlee, lying on the bed, kicked her legs up

132

with a splash of black panties under her robes. Boston thought that his brain would explode any second, along with other things. Beth sat crossed-legged in the air chair. She held her cup out to Marlee who rolled across the bed, opened the flask and poured liberally into the cup. "Sure you won't try some, hun?" she said to Boston. He nodded no and sipped some virgin Gatorade from his cup.

"It's the only way to stay sane in this place," said Beth. "If you can call anybody in this place sane." They cracked up again.

Beth was a network administrator for Barto Burgers. She sipped from her Gator-rubby and tossed a chocolate-coated coffee bean into her mouth. After a couple of loud crunches, she lifted her cup in a toast and said, "To rubby and friends...and one crazy fucking business!" They toasted and laughed.

After a few minutes, the mood simmered down and the two women sat staring vacantly at their cups, just smiling and thinking drunken thoughts. Boston broke the silence. "So you don't have any idea what the project was that Carl Rogers was working on?"

She thought a moment. Thinking seemed to bring out the sensual fullness of her lips...Boston checked his thoughts again. Beth said, "No. It was all on the hush-hush, I mean, the no-paper-trail-and-no-etrail kinda hush-hush. I've never seen that much security on a project before. We all thought it was because of the cloning leak, but this went beyond even that paranoia. It looked like a lot of senior people were out of the loop on it. I'm not sure how high up, but I'm guessing only a handful of people knew, and there was no telling who they were." She burped and giggled and Marlee whacked her on the nose with a finger as Beth tossed in another coffee bean. After a few chews, she seemed to perk up. "But the whole thing was scrapped right after Rogers' death."

"They scrapped a top secret project because one of the employees died from a heart attack?" asked Boston.

"Rogers' was one of the world's leading geneticists," said Beth. "He would have been one of the lead researchers and managers, maybe even head of research."

"He wrote two of the books I used in my doctoral research," said Marlee. "He would have played a key role in any project he worked on. But it's still a reach to close the whole thing."

"And he could still have been replaced?" said Boston.

"Yes, but not easily," said Marlee.

"Still seems strange to close the whole show over one man," said Boston.

"But that wasn't the weirdest thing," said Beth. Boston and Marlee leaned forward. Beth chewed some more and took a swig from her cup. Marlee said, "So....?"

"Oh, yeah, they shipped everybody out."

"Shipped them out?" said Boston. "Where to?"

"All over the world," said Beth.

"Just like I told you," said Marlee.

"No two went to the same place," said Beth. "They had three of us working on message and email forwarding and the addresses were everywhere. It was like they didn't want anybody talking to each other that had worked on that project. No chance to compare notes. Some weird shit's gone down in this place, but nothing as weird as that whole thing. Gave me the creeps. Especially keeping Rogers' body like that. Not even letting the family come to the funeral, if there *was* a funeral. Nobody around here was told about one. We would've seen the messaging. And then there was that other thing..." She thought for a moment as she chewed a bean.

Boston liked the way her mouth moved as she chewed. *Get away from that!* "Other thing?" he said.

"Yeah, way down below, maybe even deeper than the catacombs where Rogers is buried. They farmed out a wireless network to some company from Bangkok. Has its own dedicated routers and servers. Completely separated from the rest of the building. And the encryption is like something out of a science fiction novel. Some of that cross-dimensional computing. None of us could break it. And believe me, we tried. Whatever it is, they want it kept secret, even more so than the project Rogers was on."

"Do you know who's working on it?" asked Boston.

"No idea. Even the building security systems are useless. This project bypasses everything."

"And this came right after Rogers' death?"

"Fastest operation this company's ever pulled off. Or any other company I've ever heard of. Lotta bucks must've gone into it."

"Meaning that it would have been approved right from the top," said Marlee.

"Barto, Beaton or Toole," said Beth. "Can't think of anybody else with that much signing clout."

"You said it might be below the catacombs," said Boston.

"That's right. There was some big time excavation. Don't know how they got the dirt and rock out without it being noticed. But then, this is a big place, bigger than it looks. But maybe they just put it down there somewhere else. There was digging and stuff, though. We tracked expenses until the secure network cut us off. Then nothing."

"So there might be something underneath the catacombs?" said Boston.

"Or beside them," said Marlee.

Beth nodded and popped another bean. "And about a week ago, one of the platform techs overheard something really weird." Boston and Marlee leaned forward again. "He just heard a part of it and it wasn't too loud. He was hooking up some new equipment in Beaton's office. Toole was in there with him. They both looked mad or worried or something. Not happy. Beaton said something that sounded like 'We've got to stop him.'"

Boston and Marlee looked at each other, then at Beth, who took a big swig of lime Gator-rubby with a chocolate-coated coffee bean chaser. Boston and Marlee waited. Beth crunched and chewed.

"And?" said Boston.

"That's all," said Beth. "Just 'We've got to stop him.' No idea who they were talking about, but I'm guessing it wasn't Barto. Toole would have gone nuts all over Beaton's ass if he thought Beaton was going act on Barto in any way. The guy loved Barto like he was a big brother or something." She looked at her wristwatch. "Oh shit! I've gotta get back. I'm on night shift. Like it matters. I've been on twenty-four hour shift for weeks. But I gotta get back." She downed the rest of her drink and stood up, a bit wobbly at first, but she gained her equilibrium fast.

"You're sure you're going to be OK for work?" asked Marlee.

Beth winked. "It's the only way I know how to work in this place."

"All right then. Thanks a million," said Marlee as she stood up and gave Beth a hug. "And don't worry, we won't pass any of this along."

"I know." She frowned.

"What?" said Marlee.

"It's just that...well...I've been in your room for over an hour and I'm still in one piece, which has gotta be some kinda record. And I can't tell anybody about it."

"Oh, you little bitch," said Marlee, all smiles, and punched Beth lightly on the arm. "Like you haven't survived here before."

Beth looked at Boston. "And it was cool meeting you, Boston. Read a lot about you."

"Nice meeting you, too. And thanks."

She looked back at Marlee and said, "Keep him in one piece." And left quickly.

***

In another part of the building, eyes smoldered with hatred, a hatred aimed directly at Beth Petersen.

138

Chapter 39 - The Sweet Aroma of Sex and Rubby

Boston was amazed at the enthusiasm and energy Marlee was able to muster under the influence of enough rubbing alcohol to put an elephant into rehab.

"So my rubby breath seems to bother you less the more you get to know me," she said.

"I just pretend I'm getting a massage from a paramedic," said Boston.

She punched him in the ribs playfully. "Dickhead."

"Hey, the bruises from this afternoon haven't even stopped spreading and you're making new ones. And even the smell isn't enough to..."

Marlee grabbed his shoulder. "Don't even think about saying it!"

"OK! OK! I give!"

They lay for a while surrounded by the aroma of rubbing alcohol and sex, submerged in their own thoughts until Boston broke the silence. "Know anything about Praeder-Willi?"

"Why would you want to know about that?"

"Toole had a pile of books on it. Said they were working on it to turn off appetite but it went sour and the project was cancelled."

"That's not surprising," said Marlee.

"How so?"

"Praeder-Willi is a genetic disorder that causes people to *over* eat." As soon as the words left her mouth, she raised quickly on one elbow. Boston perked up as well.

"Toole led me to believe they were studying it to *curb* appetite."

Marlee nodded. "I guess that's not really unusual. Sometimes, you experiment with something that does the opposite of what you want to do and then work backwards to where you want to be. If they could understand how Praeder-Willi causes people to overeat, they might be able to manipulate it somehow to do the opposite. Do you think that has something to do with the deaths?"

"I saw a diary entry from Barto, made shortly before he died about something called pwx and an updated Gantt chart, but Toole said the project was scrapped a year ago."

"They might have scrapped it and somebody else might have started something similar, maybe taking another direction."

"I don't think Barto knew about it. There was a note about him wanting to find out who was on it. The rest of his journal for the next three weeks was missing. And, now that I think of it, it seemed strange that Toole would still have what looked like his Praeder-Willi research stuff still in a pile on his floor."

Marlee thought for a while and sat up. She reached for her cup and downed what was left. She pointed to a corner of her room with a pile of journals, books and binders on the floor. "From a project I was working on six months ago. Someday I'll get around to cleaning it up." Boston nodded. Marlee continued. "And unless they've made some

140

really big quantum leaps in genetic science in the last year, I don't see how Praeder could be used to kill people. It's a genetic disorder. It's hardwired right into the genes. You would have to alter the genetic structure of the victim to make it work. Even if it were possible to do something like that to an adult human being, it would take years. Do you have any idea how complex the human genome is?"

"OK," said Boston. "Let's leave that one alone for the time being. The last part of the note...find out who's on it. Who would be on something like that?"

Marlee laughed and took a swig straight from her flask. "In a company where they're cloning food? Just about anybody. Like Beth said, there's projects going on here that nobody knows about. And I'll bet there's research personnel who've written textbooks on every aspect of genetics and cloning who might be considered celebrities, but might be in this building as we speak, and nobody knows about it." She recapped her flask and rolled toward Boston, pushing her right leg between his legs and curling up into him. "And by the way, we're in."

"Gabby's getting us into the catacombs?"

"Almost a VIP pass."

"A VIP pass," said Boston, smiling. "Sounds impressive. What do we get for a VIP pass?"

Marlee bounced up and mounted Boston. "It starts off with..."

Chapter 40 - Night Chills

Thick fog swirled around Boston as he plied through the port city night. Downtown Saint John wasn't just quiet, it was one of the darkest places on Earth. Desolate. This was the center of the city and there was no one around. Sure, it was almost three in the morning, but it was still the center of the city and every city had its nocturnal life. There were no dogs or cats, no drunks. This had been a bustling port city before the fog had taken over. Where were the rats?

And what the hell was he doing?

He knew that he was getting in over his head on this referral, but that was his style. He'd done it throughout his career and he was good at it. He'd been in to the point of drowning in his own sense of being untouchable. But then, wasn't he the great Boston Jonson, CI Extraordinaire?

But there was something different this time. It wasn't that he was sleeping with someone who could, after all, be a suspect. He was good at that too. And it wasn't the novelty of the murders-and murders they were. Two men eating themselves to death within a day of each other was more than just a passing virus, even though global warming *had* spawned a variety of strange new illnesses. Boston could sense the intent surrounding the deaths, and he was certain that Kemper was killed because he was trying to tell him something.

And Kemper had been afraid of Bethany. Was she involved somehow? She was a corporate lackey who probably would have sold her soul for a promotion-or a mirror-but could she murder someone? And when would she have had the opportunity to kill him? She'd been with Boston with the exception of just over an hour. It was more likely that Kemper was already toothpicking himself to death while Bethany was still with him.

And according to Marlee, it was impossible to use any of the technologies Barto Burger was working on to make someone overeat to the point of self-destruction. Toole had said that Praeder-Willi Syndrome had been a dead end and was abandoned, but there seemed to be a lot of unknown experiments going on in The Spit, and a lot of warring at the top.

And why was Beaton not putting the screws to Boston's bosses to get him taken off the referral immediately? He had the clout, but he was letting Boston have until tomorrow for a referral that would normally have been finished within the first hour that he'd arrived on the scene if he hadn't had to speak to Toole in the next morning. But he hadn't really needed to speak to Toole, had he?

And why was he taking so long? Why not just refer to the shrinks or the police? What the hell was he doing?

He suspected he would find answers tomorrow in the catacombs. Marlee had outdone herself-VIP passes, special eye print signatures that bypassed security. Nobody would ever know that Marlee and Boston had been in the catacombs.

The catacombs.

Again, Boston felt a chill deep down where his soul vibrated.

***

NO! NO! NO! She screamed in her thoughts. *NO!* But she couldn't stop eating.

Chapter 41 - Lemon Pie And Coffee In The Oldest Incorporated City In Canada

The kitchen in the Twin Boar Bed and Breakfast was exactly like the dining room, a relic from a long ago past, but then, everything in this city seemed spewed out of the timeless mists that surrounded it like a sodden cocoon.

"We've some of the best examples of Victorian architecture in this part of the world, you know, Mr. Jonson," said Mrs. Orange. "It was on account of the great fire of 1877, Black Wednesday they called it. Burned for nine hours and took with it much of the downtown. Twenty-seven million dollars in damage, it did. And that, sir, would have been a lot more then than it was today." She poured steaming coffee into an oversized plain white cup as Boston wiped crumbs from his lips with a cloth napkin.

"Entire insurance companies went bankrupt and bank assets went up in smoke, you know."

"I can imagine that the people here would have a lot of pride in a city with as much historical background as Saint John."

"Oldest incorporated city in Canada, you know."

Boston tried his luck. "It must have been quite a cultural shock when they tore down so much of that history."

Mrs. Orange's lips curled into a small frown. Holding the coffee pot in one hand, she wiped the huge wooden table with a white and blue checkered kitchen towel with the other, even though the tabletop was immaculate. Boston cut off another wedge of lemon meringue pie with his fork and lifted it slowly to his mouth. It was the most delicious pie he'd ever eaten and he was going to savor every bite.

Mrs. Orange shrugged her shoulders. "We don't talk about it much," she said. "But, yes, it was more than a wee bit of a shock to folks here. The fog was here first, but it won't last. People like to think that when it lifts, the old city will be back. Things will be back to normal. But not with that building taking up the whole harbor area. No sir, not with The Spit and all its confounded gargoyles haunting the place."

"Haunting the place?"

"People hear strange noises coming from high up around the building late at night. They're somewhere up there, popping up here in the fog, popping up there."

"You don't really believe there's ghosts up there, do you Mrs. Orange?"

She smiled. "You finish up our pie now, Mr. Jonson. It's getting late." With that, she shuffled to the counter, put the coffee pot on a ceramic pot stand, hung up the towel and shuffled out of the kitchen through a swinging door.

"Thank you, Mrs. Orange," he called after her.

As Boston finished his pie and coffee, he thought about the feelings the Barto Burger headquarters must have generated in this city, as though the place had been built on hatred. And now people were dying in it.

On a condiment tray by his pie plate, a small pewter container brimmed with toothpicks.

***

In The Spit, Marlee Dunn snorted quietly and turned on her side without waking up. This was observed by an eye in a peephole where a dark wooden strut disappeared into the wall. The eye disappeared and a piece of wood slid over the hole like the shutter closing on a camera lens.

Chapter 42 - The Well-Practiced Smile

"But why can't I fuck him?"

"What would be the purpose?" said the raspy voice beyond the intricate carvings and meaningless patterns.

Bethany squinted her eyes, trying to peer through the dark mesh of the screen. "I might learn something. He might talk about things on his mind that he might not say in less intimate circumstances. You wouldn't believe the things men tell me when…"

An awkward silence hung in the air over Bethany and the space between her and the confessional, but it lifted quickly and Bethany composed herself and frowned. She ran her fingers across the bottom of her neck, wiping dampness from the surface of well-lotioned skin.

"I'm sure I wouldn't want to know," said the voice.

Bethany scowled. She hated the voice. It was always so right, so aggravating, and so much in control. She hated being controlled. That was supposed to end. She was supposed to have complete control over her life by now. That was the promise.

Candles mounted on wood and brass poles flickered and cast wavering light on the stone walls. Sometimes candlelight was romantic, sometimes it was just spooky. The light in this room was hopeless.

"He's such a smart ass," she said.

"We've always known that," said the voice.

"He knows more than he's letting on."

"It doesn't matter. There's nothing he can do to stop us."

"The Dunn woman is helping him."

"Then, God help him."

Bethany wasn't laughing at the joke. She never laughed. It was something she observed in others and dismissed as anything that could have any relevance in her own life. The most she could handle was a well-practiced smile, complete with dimples. "She brought a friend to talk to him."

"We know this," said the voice. "It's been taken care of."

Bethany cocked her head. "How did you...?"

"We know these things," said the voice. "You know that."

She nodded slowly. "Yes. I know that."

"Now, get sleep. You need sleep."

"Easy to say. But I've been drinking coffee all day."

"Two cups. You've had two cups."

"That's all?"

"You need sleep."

Sitting in her small wooden chair, Bethany's shoulders slumped, her eyes closed, her face relaxed, and she snored.

***

Boston's wallet woke him at 5:30 AM, an hour after he'd finally drifted off to sleep.

"How soon can you get to the Barto Burger building?" asked Laurel.

150

Chapter 43 - A Dark Foreboding Place

It was a dark foreboding place, a strange place where ceilings soared into heights where wooden beams and fixtures formed indiscernible patterns. Arched windows set in the stone walls wasted glass on the usual depressing panorama of unrelenting clouds of fog. Shoulder-length dividers sectioned off workspaces just like in most tech departments in most modern office buildings, except these dividers were made of hard blunt wood. The workspaces contained wooden desks and chairs that might have been lifted out of a fifteenth-century monastery. Wafer thin screens from the most advanced computers in the world formed bubbles of blue light around each of the workspaces. But the overall effect was one of gloom, made still gloomier through the sunglasses Boston wore to cover his two black eyes. Even his fresh blue Hawaiian shirt wasn't enough to brighten the scene.

Beth Petersen was slumped over her desk, dark fluids flowing out of her mouth onto the desktop. The light from her computer spread an eerie glow over her wide-open eyes and shocked expression. Bags of Free Trade chocolate-coated coffee beans littered her desk, some of them ripped open and spilling beans onto the desk and floor.

Boston looked around at the dark robed figures sitting at their desks gazing at their screens. "And nobody noticed this happening?" he asked.

"It would appear that way," said Beaton, enunciating painfully slow.

"She ate herself to death on chocolate-coated coffee beans and nobody heard anything, nobody noticed anything strange, and nobody thought that maybe they should do something when she obviously started gagging?"

"The people in this room are, of course, very busy and intent on their work, Mr. Jonson." Beaton's slow speaking fish mouth was seriously getting on Boston's nerves. "It's not unusual for them to work for hours completely unaware of their surroundings or the passage of time."

Boston stared at the lifeless body that had excited his thoughts just hours ago. He could still hear her laughter and the drunken slur of her voice. He couldn't imagine how this could have happened with people no more than fifteen feet away and nobody had noticed a thing. He'd questioned them all and gotten nothing but blank stares and disinterest. *Was she the only human in this place?* And most of them had packages of coffee beans on their desks. They seemed to be a staple in his place. But no one had noticed Beth Petersen ripping into several dozen bags and gulping them down by the handful. *God*, he thought, *that much caffeine that fast. Which came first, a heart attack or death by overeating?*

And there was something different about Beaton, something in his eyes and general demeanor, a lack of the smug confidence that surrounded him earlier. He was still an insufferable ass, but there was something in his eyes, something like worry maybe? Or was it fear? Was Beaton afraid of something? Afraid of the shit that another suspicious death would stir up? Afraid of the press that Barto Burger would get when it became public that three people in the headquarters building had eaten themselves to death? No, he was too smug in his power to be afraid of that. And just who would he have to answer to for the bad PR? For all intents and purposes, he was the numero uno in the organization now. Or was he? Boston would have to look into that.

"What are you afraid of?" he asked.

Beaton's eyes flashed as he sucked air through his round little mouth. He glared at Boston as he let it out slowly like air seeping out of a punctured tire. "I can have you off this, Mr. Jonson, off this...and in more pain than you can quite..."

"Then do it."

"What?"

"Do it," said Boston, smirking brazenly. "Have me taken off the referral. You can do it anytime you want. So do it."

Beaton's fury seemed to flash out in the space around him, like a solar flare threatening to burn everything in its path. His nose and mouth trembled. His eyes widened and rounded. His fists clenched. His six and a half feet of solid mass quivered like angry pudding. He let out a long gust of breath, turned and stomped away.

Boston could swear that he felt the stone floor vibrate with each of the big man's steps. *Time to speed things up.*

Chapter 44 - Messing With Powerful People

It was probably a blessing for Marlee to still be half in the bag on rubbing alcohol. Her black hair was wild and tangled and her eyes red and swollen. "I can't believe it," she said through quick deep breaths, the kind that come with not knowing whether to scream or cry. "She was just here a few hours ago. We were all laughing. We were drinking Gatorade cocktails. She was helping us." Her mouth opened wide and she looked straight into Boston's eyes. "That was it, wasn't it? She was killed wasn't she? She was killed because she was helping us, wasn't she?" She shook her head from side to side as tears spilled over her red cheeks.

Boston pulled her head to his shoulder and they sat on her bed. She was limp in his arms except for the wracking in her chest as she sobbed. After a few minutes, the sobbing stopped, the wracking stopped, her body stiffened and she raised her head. She was a mess, but her face practically vibrated with anger. "They killed her. We have to get them. You know they killed her. And now they have to pay. Beth was the closest friend I had in this place, the only one I spent time with just getting..." A fit of sobs grabbed her. After a few minutes, it passed and the grief in her eyes turned to anger. "How do we get them, CI guy? Tell me how we get them?"

"First," said Boston, "you need a cold shower. Then we'll talk."

***

While Marlee showered, Boston talked to his wallet. "So there haven't been any requests to have me taken off this referral?"

"There was a lot of talk about making you speed things up, but no, nothing about actually taking you off. Why? Who have you pissed off now, Boston?"

"Obviously nobody," he said. "And you said there was no talk about reassigning me? I thought there were people in high places getting pissed off at me."

"There were. And it looked bad. You're messing with some really powerful people there, dear. It looked as though they were going to have your balls fricasseed, but everything seems to have calmed down. But then, it's been less than a day. I'm sure you'll get things stirred up again, won't you?"

"Oh, come on now, Laurel, you know me."

"Exactly," she said, and the tiny wallet screen went blank.

Why the hell hasn't Beaton done anything yet. What's he up to?

Chapter 45 - In the Room of the Nano Masseuse

The Spit's cafeteria was almost as crowded in the morning as it had been the previous afternoon. Shift workers, thought Boston. It was still eerily hushed for a place where people congregated on their free time.

"Maybe it's just me," he said, "but shouldn't there be more noise in this place with a couple hundred people slurping down cloned junk food and talking?"

"Nano sound buffers," said Marlee. She was looking much better after a cold shower and a quickie followed by a hot shower. "They float around in the air and massage the sound waves into something quieter."

Boston thought about this. "Massage the sound waves?" Maybe that was why he couldn't pick up on the vibrations in this place. If the nanos were all over the building then…but that wouldn't explain the hundreds of other times he'd been unable to pick up on them. Someday, though. It would come to him.

"We just call it a massage," she said, "because the science behind something like that-just the concept of millions of tiny molecular robots buzzing invisibly around your head while you eat-would drive most people crazy."

"Massage does it for me, then. How're you feeling now?" He reached over the narrow bench and cupped his hands around hers.

"Better. Thanks. I'm going to miss her. We spent a lot of time getting plastered together. Now I just want to get the people who killed her." Her face was calm, but her eyes, those big brown eyes with their forever brows, burned brightly with resolute anger. If she were the jinx everybody feared she was, that anger would be a formidable force. "Are you afraid of me?" she asked.

Boston raised his brows. "Afraid of you?"

"The way you're looking at me. It's...I'm not sure..."

"Just thinking that I wouldn't want Hurricane Marlee after..."

She kicked him under the table. "Ouch!"

"So what's the plan?"

Boston reached under the table and rubbed his shin as he spoke. "This has gone beyond anything that comes remotely under the heading of Standard Referral. This is turning into a full-scale investigation, and that's not really my mandate."

"But it's what you seem to do a lot of."

"And then there's that."

"So what do you usually do when a referral gets out of control?"

"I didn't say it was out of control." He sat up. "That shin's going to be as black as my eyes."

"Sorry. I'll try to go easy on you in the future." She smiled, leaned over the bench, and kissed him on the lips.

Boston gripped her hands again. "Forgiven. And I guess the next step is to get into the catacombs."

"What do you think we'll find there?"

"I don't know. We need to see Carl Rogers' body, see how he died. I'm guessing it wasn't a heart attack."

"Sounds grim," said Marlee, as she sipped from a porcelain cup filled with coffee and rubbing alcohol.

"It will be."

"By the way, where's your little guide?"

"Bethany? I haven't seen her. Maybe I've lost my guide privileges."

***

In the small room, by the confessional, Bethany woke with a start, her eyes wide, her face stark, her cup empty.

Chapter 46 - One Good Reason for Taking the Stairs

Another damn set of stairs. Cracked and crumbling, these were even more worn than the ones leading to the infirmary and they seemed just as infinite, though they were necessary if they wanted to keep their visit to the catacombs secret. The elevators were monitored, as were the stairs leading to the infirmary. Boston almost tripped over a jagged chunk of rubble. *What idiot architect deliberately created a mess like this in a damn stairway?* The steps under their feet this time were used by only a handful of executives in The Spit, and apparently led to surprising places that only the top level executives might ever want to visit-and visit without being seen.

"Barto, Toole and a few others are the only ones who've ever used this passage," said Marlee. "Can you see well enough with those sunglasses on? And I'm so sorry about that, my poor little CI sex slave."

"Knock it off," said Boston with a smirk widening below his UV eyes.

"What?" said Marlee.

"You're not walking in front of me."

"Who said I wanted to walk in front of you. Although, I *am* supposed to be taking *you* to the catacombs."

"You *are* taking me…back seat driver style."

"You're a shit head, you know that?"

"I'm a shit head wearing sunglasses in a dimly lit stairwell made of stone somewhere in the bowels of a city that's been in fog longer than a third of the population's been alive. You're the relish on my hotdog, Mar, but I feel just a little safer in front of you." Suddenly he had a thought. "By the way, elevators seem to open up in the walls all over this place. How come you made me walk up all those stairs to the infirmary while I was bleeding to death?"

"Really want to know?"

"Yes. Really."

"I wanted you to get a good long look at my ass."

"And just what was that supposed to accomplish?"

"Hey, hon, what did you have for lunch yesterday?"

"Good point, and by the way…nice ass."

Marlee smiled, tripped, and banged her forehead into the back of Boston's head.

***

Where the hell is he? And the Dunn woman's gone too. Then she remembered. *Oh right, the catacombs. Perfect.*

Chapter 47 - A Dank Not So Well-Lighted Place

The door they closed behind them must have weighed half a ton. Constructed of thick hardwood beams strapped together with solid brass plating and mounted on inch thick brass hinges, Boston was surprised at how easily it swung. Well oiled, even though it creaked.

"Quaint," he said.

"The architect who designed this place was from Germany," said Marlee. "I heard that he had a weird sense of humor."

"I can believe that." Boston looked around at the room they'd just entered. "Holy shit. Is this place real?"

"The real thing," said Marlee. "Every block of stone and scrap of wood in this place was imported from European castles and monasteries. It cost millions just in transportation costs."

He could believe that too. The place was cavernous, like monstrously huge giant's den carved into the bowels of the earth. High rib-vaulted ceilings formed a conical ceiling from some ancient past. Age mottled stone walls flickered and danced in the dim light from hundreds of tarnished brass torches. The smell of fuel was heavy in the air. So was the smell of mildew and wood rot, and the smell was probably real in this place.

The floor was lined with row after row of dark granite sarcophagi, hundreds of them. They disappeared into the darkness at the far end of the chamber.

"All this for Carl Rogers?" asked Boston.

"Only if they buried him in pieces. Lots of tiny pieces."

"What the hell is this place?"

"Just another great weirdness in the Barto Burger Empire. You come to expect things like this the longer you work here."

They walked slowly toward the rows of stone structures closest to them. "You're sure there's nobody in here?" said Boston.

"Gabby said nobody ever comes down here."

"Except to bury Carl Rogers."

"Except for that."

As they came within a few feet of the nearest sarcophagus, Marlee let out a tight gasp.

"What?" said Boston.

She pointed at a brass plate with an inscription attached to the side of the big stone body jar. It read:

Bradley Alexander Parks

"You know him?"

"Yes."

"Sorry. I didn't ..."

"He's not dead."

Chapter 48 - A Spooky Place to Rest in Peace

"I guess that would explain why there's no date," said Boston. He walked over to another sarcophagus. "Thomas Glen Mitchell. Know him?"

"Works in the marketing department. Nice guy, but a bit of a flake. And very much alive."

"Again, no date."

"What's going on here," said Marlee. The flask was out. "Care for a nip?"

"Much as I'm beginning to understand how that stuff probably fits in well here, I think I'll pass for now."

"Your choice, lover." She took two swallows while Boston checked out a few more inscriptions. "Any dates yet?" she asked.

"Nada."

Marlee walked slowly in the opposite direction, reading the names, shaking her head. "All these people are still alive." She craned her neck toward one of the granite body bags to her right and squinted her eyes. "Don't know this one, but no date. Must still be alive."

Boston joined her in front of the unknown name. "Name doesn't ring any bells at all?"

"There's a lot of people working in his building. They wear robes and hoods. I wouldn't even know if I had passed ... let's see ..." She looked closely at a brass plate. "... J. Richard Jacobs in the hall a dozen times every day, let alone know his name." She shivered visibly. "This place gives me the creeps."

Boston looked over the rows of stone structures. "So he could be somebody who works here?"

"Probably is."

"There's hundreds of them." He thought a moment. "One for everybody who works here?"

Marlee shivered again. "Our contracts allow them to keep our bodies for burial here, if we work in headquarters. I don't think anybody ever took that seriously until after Carl Rogers' death." Her eyes widened. "It was in *my* contract." Her face paled. "There's one of these down here for me, isn't there?"

"I'm guessing, yes," said Boston, looking over the rows of vacant death beds in the flame-lit gloom. "But we need to find the one with Carl Rogers' body in it. Unless you want to find yours."

She shook her head no. "I'll pass on that. I'm getting low," she said, tapping the flask under her robe with a sharp metallic *clenck*. "So how do we find Rogers? There's a lot of area to cover here."

"We start walking."

"Boston, sweetheart?"

"Yes."

"If you find one with my name on it …"

"Yes."

"I really mean it, keep it to yourself."

Chapter 49 - Carl Kingsley Rogers (2041 - 2069)

"Here it is!" They'd scoured the rows of sarcophagi for about twenty minutes before Marlee came across the only one with a date ...

Carl Kingsley Rogers
2041 - 2069

Boston was three rows away and about thirty feet behind her. He'd tried to tap into the vibrations in this place for about a minute, loosening his mind, emptying his thoughts into the universal void, relaxing his shoulders and letting his head slump forward a bit, breathing in the dankness of the air, savoring the bits and pieces of ancient civilizations that had been imported to this place from all over Europe, catching a glimpse of Marlee's ass as she pulled ahead of him a few rows over...that swagger, that sway...

So much for vibrations.

"At least it wasn't at the end of the room," said Boston as he stepped up beside Marlee. He looked past Rogers' tomb at the rows spreading beyond his vision and wondered at the almost impossible job it must have been to excavate this place. *Where did they put the dirt and rock?* He looked at Rogers' burial plate. "He was only twenty-eight years old."

"If you don't excel in this business early, you get buried professionally very fast."

"No pun intended?"

Marlee thought, grimaced. "I should have brought an extra flask."

"You may be right," said Boston stepping closer to the sarcophagus and inspecting it. "I think the top slides off."

Marlee's laugh was gruff but light and bouncy and completely out of place in the ponderous solemnity surrounding them. "This isn't *really* medieval Europe," she said. "I don't think the people who put Rogers' body in there would be the type to be pushing a hundred or more pounds of granite around."

"Your point? Dear."

"Don't get snarky with me, CI guy. I'm just telling you..." She paused for effect. "There has to be a button somewhere."

After a few minutes examining every inch of granite surface, Boston said, "Time for brute force." He pushed the stone plate on top. Nothing happened. He tried pushing from the other side. Nothing. He tried both ends. "Maybe they glued it in place." A light patch of sweat darkened the blue and green palm trees on his shirt.

Marlee kicked the base of the sarcophagus lightly. "Nobody around her expends more energy than is absolutely necessary," she said. "There has to be an easy way to do this, something involving automation, and probably something obvious."

"Obvious?"

"Geniuses are notorious for forgetting anything that doesn't relate directly to their work. There has to be something..." She closed her mouth and watched Boston's hand move, her expression one of ah-yes-that.

He pressed his finger on the brass nameplate and the top of the sarcophagus lifted up and away from them with a slow pneumatic swish.

"Oh God," said Marlee, "That's just too much."

Chapter 50 - Somehow Another Murder

"I'd forgotten that about him," said Marlee, staring through a glass cover over Carl Rogers' perfectly preserved body. "Even when he was walking through the halls or sitting in the cafeteria-he chewed his nails."

Whatever he was in life-genius, prodigy, anti-social geek, son of grieving parents, nail chewer-in death he was the embodiment of those few seconds of dread just before waking from a dream where the unnamed and the unseen are just about to stop your heart by revealing themselves. His face was white, his pop-eyes wide and round and staring straight ahead. Shreds of skin dangled from his lips. The flesh from his left arm had been chewed off almost up to the elbow. The white death-soured skin above the amputation bore the unmistakable imprint of tooth marks. Human tooth marks.

Carl Rogers had died eating his own arm.

"Probably bled to death," said Boston.

"But how could anybody do something like that?" Marlee shook her head as if to say no to what she was seeing. If possible, her skin paled still further.

"How could anybody eat himself to death on hamburgers?" said Boston. "Or with toothpicks or coffee beans? Somebody made them do it. Somebody murdered them."

"But it's not possible," she was still shaking her head.

"No, Marlee. It is possible. Somebody made it possible."

"But the science behind this..."

"You said Praeder-Willi is an appetite enhancer..."

"Nothing on this planet enhances appetite like this," she said, pointing at Carl Rogers' remains. "Praeder-Willi is genetic. People are born with it. It takes years for it to kill people through obesity with things like heart attacks, strokes, diabetes..."

"But they can eat themselves to death."

Marlee lifted her hands and shrugged. "It's rare, but there have been cases where people with Praeder have gorged themselves till their stomachs burst, but that's on food. Nobody eats his own arm off with Praeder-Willi. This is something completely different. This is completely off the charts."

"This is real, Marlee. This is..." Boston put a finger to his mouth and looked warily around the room. Marlee began to speak. He put a finger to her lips and shook his head no. They stood motionless, listening. There was no sound in the catacombs but the sound of their own breathing and the occasional *whump whump* of a torch adjusting its flame.

"What?" whispered Marlee after a minute.

Boston shook his head. "I don't know. Thought I heard something."

"Now this place is really giving me the creeps. Can we leave?"

"We need to come back here," said Boston. "Beth said something about a huge project down here. Under this place or beside it."

"You've gotta be kidding," said Marlee, petulantly. "It could take ages to find it."

"Whatever's going on around here," said Boston, "that room is the key to it all." He touched Rogers' nameplate again and the lid swished down and closed with a muffled thud. "We better get back upstairs. Bethany's probably having a fit trying to find me. And don't you have to get to work?"

"Ever hear of flex hours?"

***

Damn it, she thought. She'd almost given herself away. She should have known better than to underestimate Boston Jonson. Fool or not, he didn't seem to miss much. She waited till they started walking before she twisted the bottom of the brass torch by her head. The stone blocks beside her slid noiselessly inward forming a door in the wall.

Too late to get them this time, she thought. *Next time*.

Chapter 51 - A Sudden Realization

"No, forget it," said Boston, as he climbed the steps they'd taken down to the catacombs. "Much as I would love to stare at your ass all the way up these steps, I'm not going to let you smash my sunglasses with the back of your head."

"But my forehead is just as sore as the back of your head from on the way down. I'm sharing the pain, luv."

"Stare at *my* ass for a while."

"Your loss."

They climbed for a few minutes not saying anything as Boston thought about Rogers' body with its half-eaten arm. There was something about it that bothered him, something other than the grisly way he'd died. Marlee, following closely, tried to decide on whether to give his ass an eight or a nine.

"You know..." said Boston.

"Eight," said Marlee. She put her left pinky finger to her lower lip, creased her brows in thought, and said, "No, maybe nine."

"What are you...?"

"I'm giving you a nine. I'm very picky."

Boston chuckled. "Thanks. I suppose I should feel honored."

"Naw, just feel terribly indebted. But you can make it up to me in the sack when we get back upstairs. You were going to say something?"

"I was thinking about Rogers' body."

"And you don't want to stare at my ass all the way up these stairs. I'm beginning to wonder about you, lover."

"I'm serious. There's something wrong, or weird, or something. I can't put my finger on it."

"On what?"

"On whatever I can't put my finger on!"

"Hey! Don't get snarkey again. I don't even know what you're..." She opened her mouth, stared at the wall, thinking. She started to speak, but shook her head.

"What?" said Boston. He stopped climbing and turned to face her.

She looked up at him, mouth still open. "Uh...it's...I think I might have an idea what's weird about his body." She thought a moment longer. "It's been preserved. Why would they preserve his body?"

Boston's face lit up. "You're right! There's no reason to preserve a body, unless..."

"Unless they want to use it." She opened her mouth slowly, eyes widening. "They're saving his tissue. They're going to clone him."

"And they have boxes for everybody in the building."

"They're going to clone the whole damn head office."

"Maybe not. Toole said something about closing down a project because of legal implications or something."

"And?"

"And that was all. Bethany was there. Put the kibosh on Toole tout suite."

"Self-indulgent little bitch."

"And no swagger."

"No what?"

172

"Nothing. But that might have been the project he was talking about. With the Rogers family lawyers breathing down their necks, they might have abandoned the whole thing."

"Nobody abandons anything around here if it can make money. And they're not squeamish about how they treat people. Dead or alive."

"Do you think you can get Gabby to find out where the place Beth talked about is located? Maybe get us in?"

"I can try, but I can't promise. Gabby's no big fan of the status quo around here, but with Barto gone, all the balances of power are shaky at best."

"I'll treat you to lunch."

"Done!"

Chapter 52 - Liar, Liar

The smile on Bethany's lips vibrated and the slow controlled tenor of her voice couldn't hide the fury stomping out a war dance in her eyes. She was pissed.

"Well, Mr. Jonson, I certainly hope your morning had been fruitful. I've only been waiting here for two hours and twenty-three minutes."

"I wasn't aware that we were supposed to meet here." Adding an hour to the time Bethany had waited, it had been only a little short of three and a half hours in which Boston and Marlee had been to the catacombs and rushed up to her quarters for a quickie before he came to the main hall to meet Bethany while Marlee went to see Gabby.

"Well, I just assumed…"

"You're not angry are you?"

It took her nearly a minute before she calmed enough to answer. "No. No, why would I be angry? Just a misunderstanding. This is usually where visitors and personnel meet." She drew a sweeping motion with her right arm to take in the main hall, which was more crowded than it had been the day before with tourists and robed employees scuttling about. "So where were you?"

"Checking things out."

"Checking things out?"

"Yes, checking things out. Yesterday, you said something about Dr. Toole not being happy about something happening again. You said you would get back to me on that."

Bethany sipped loudly from her cup, eyes darting around. Maybe looking around the main hall for something to change the topic? She finished sipping, looked Boston straight in the eyes and said, "I think you might be mistaken, Mr. Jonson. I don't recall saying anything about something happening again and if I did, I was very likely mistaken. And didn't we already go through this yesterday?"

Boston nodded. "In other words, you're not going to tell me."

"There's nothing to tell."

"Fine. I'd like to speak to Peters."

Chapter 53 - Capitalist Corporations

Peters' office was like the rest of The Spit, stone and heavy wood. Boston wondered if the people who worked here ever got the feudal-Europe-still-kickin-around-in-the-twenty-first-century blues. Then he thought about the amount of rubbing alcohol that must have been consumed in The Spit in the course of a month. Probably not enough.

Peters wasn't happy. In fact, he looked outright worried. Bethany was pissed. The looks passing between the two were the stuff of Theater of the Absurd.

Boston loved it.

After a short call on her cell instructing her to cooperate completely with Boston's referral, including confidential information, even without non-disclosures, Bethany hadn't said a word all the way up to Peters' office. Boston could probably have popped corn on her forehead.

"Yes, Mr. Peters," said Boston. "You have to answer the question."

Peters looked again at Bethany, panic in his eyes and his voice. "But that's ridiculous! The project doesn't even exist! How can I tell him who had signing authority for something that doesn't even exist?"

Bethany didn't say a thing. She glared at Boston. He imagined corn popping in her mouth, her cheeks bulging with popcorn rage. He almost smiled. "OK," he said. "Let me reword the question." He stood up and walked to the side of Peters' desk, put his hands on the varnished surface and leaned forward, bringing his face within inches of Peters' face. Peters looked terrified, his eyes zipping between Boston and Bethany. He kept trying to say something, but nothing came out. "Let's just pretend there's a top secret project going on at the bottom of this building, somewhere in the vicinity of the catacombs. Somebody had to provide whoever was in charge with the materials they needed. That would be you."

"No!" Peters' eyes were round. "It could have been anybody! The chain of command has been nuts in this place for almost a year."

"But you made sure that everybody had what they needed on the Praeder-Willi project?"

The blood drained out of Peters' face. "How...how did you...?"

"Somebody did the research, you did the administering, right?"

"But it was scrapped a year ago. It was a disaster. The whole thing was closed down."

"But what if there were another project-a project so secret that virtually nobody here knew about it-started, say, three months ago. And let's suppose you didn't know anything about it. Who would have had authorization rights to make that project happen?"

Peters glanced desperately at Bethany, but she ignored him. She was looking at her reflection in the mirrored surface of a plaque on Peters' desk. From the look in her eyes, though, Boston guessed that her thoughts were packed with murder. The knuckles folded around her coffee cup were white.

Finally, Peters broke. "It would have been somebody at the top. Not one of the department heads. Somebody in executive management. The lower levels of the building are highly classified. Access is restricted to about ten people-Mr. Barto, Dr. Toole, Mr. Beaton, Dr. Brunner, Gabby Pinches ..."

"Gabby Pinches is that senior?" said Boston.

"For all her red-neck appearance and talk, she's actually a brilliant scientist and one of the first to come on board with Mr. Barto and Dr. Toole." Peters relaxed a little, color began to return to his face and the look of desperation evaporated from his eyes. "She was in on all the major early decisions. Mr. Barto trusted her, and he was rarely one to trust others. But I doubt that she would have had anything to do with the kind of project you're describing. It doesn't sound like her. And there's one other thing..." He glanced quickly at Bethany, who was still fixed on her reflection. In fact, it was almost creepy. She seemed to be in another world, completely oblivious of anyone else in the room.

"One other thing?" prompted Boston.

"The top three senior execs can authorize department heads to do just about anything. This isn't a democracy or a government, Mr. Jonson. This is a capitalist corporation that exists to make money. They do what they have to do to that end. Your theoretical project could have come from anywhere. But I swear this is the first I've heard about it."

178

Boston straightened up. Peters slumped in his chair. Bethany stared vacantly at her reflection. "I think it's time to talk to Gabby Pinches again," said Boston.

Chapter 54 - Too Old To Be A Hero

It was like Bethany was a mile away. She hadn't said a word all the way down to the labs where Gabby worked. She hadn't even looked at her thousands of reflections in the elevator, just sipped from her empty cup, staring at some perplexing non-object a few feet beyond her gaze. Boston almost felt sorry for her.

Even in the huge vault-ceiling lab where Gabby worked it wasn't hard to immediately pick out the tawny old scientist, first by her boisterous voice and hacking cough, then by the crabbed body under the light blue robe

She saw Boston and smiled, signed an e-pad, handed it to a faceless brown robe, and walked surprisingly straight to meet Boston and Bethany. "Betcha never thought you'd get yer CI curls up in such a braid as this, did ya, Jonson?"

Boston smiled. "Things seem to be heating up around here. Got time for a few questions?"

"Always got time for a good lookin' man with orange hair an' a bright blue Maui Woowee shirt." She laughed and hacked. "What can I do for ya, Jonson?" She motioned him and Bethany toward an island of wooden chairs around a thick wooden coffee table at the end of a lab desk. "Sit your asses down for a while an' let's talk."

Gabby and Boston sat. Bethany stood, still miles away.

"What's got that girl's ass a-twitter?"

Boston, noticing the comment just bouncing off the still vacant Bethany. "Too much coffee, I suppose."

Gabby mumbled something and hacked. "What's on your mind, Jonson?"

"We were just talking to Peters. We know about the Praeder-Willi project." Gabby whistled and coughed. "And there might have been something else started a few months ago, a project secret enough that only a handful of people might have the authority to authorize it, might have given someone else authorization rights."

Bethany suddenly reached into her robe and took out her phone. She walked away from the two and talked for a few seconds and-without even looking at Boston-walked away and disappeared into the wall elevator.

"That girl's gettin' weirder all the time," said Gabby. "Never much cared for her. But don't let that signin' authority thing take you too far outta yer ball game. Peters is a corporate ass-kisser. He'll throw smoke all over the damn place just to confuse you." She leaned closer to him. "By the way, that Marlee girl's bin bonin' you, ain't she?"

Boston could feel himself begin to blush.

Gabby winked, smiled and hacked. "Don't worry 'bout me. I like the girl. Like you too. 'S why I helped you pair get into the catacombs. Marlee says you gotta go back. Gotta death wish or somethin', Jonson? People are gettin' murdered around here, you know?"

"I know. And with increasing frequency, it seems. So you don't think it was anybody other than somebody at the top who authorized whatever this top secret thing is?"

"Don't know. Could be anythin'. Just sayin'... don't trust Peters, or anybody around here for that matter."

"Not even you?" Boston smiled.

Gabby smiled back. "I could tell you a few things make your head spin about ol' Gabby Pinches."

"So what's going on around here, then?"

"Lots. Lots a stuff that don't make no sense. Other that does. There's a war goin' on here."

"So I heard."

"Ain't heard the half of it. Nobody has. All sorts of things goin' on an' people disappearin'..."

"Disappearing?"

"Buncha scientists, big shot scientists, in here a few months ago-prob'ly around the same time as your top secret project. Saw some of 'em briefly in the main hall. Thought they might be visitin' till I saw their luggage arrive later."

"How did you know it was theirs?"

After a short laugh, a long hacking cough and a deep breath that almost triggered another fit, she smiled and said, "Got my ways." She winked. "But these were big timers, Nobel laureates, an' leading researchers, nano-people an' brain specialists. Saw 'em just the once, an' then they was gone. Read the e-rags. Some of 'em are missin'. Nobody seems to know nothin'."

"Shouldn't you have reported any of this?"

"To who?"

"Well..."

"There's a war goin' on in this place, Jonson. People are disappearin' an' now people are bein' murdered. I'm too old to be a hero."

"Sorry." He shrugged. "You're right. So why are you spilling the beans now?"

"Let's just say I gotta feelin' the beans have started spillin' all over the place since you got here. Won't take long before you crack open the whole bag."

"I wish I had your confidence."

She pointed toward the wall where Bethany had gone into the elevator. "You seem to have made your mark on the little trollop. Ain't never seen her lose her cool like that."

"I don't think she liked the idea of me getting blanket access access to anything I want."

"Anythin'?"

"Apparently so. She got the call just before we met with Peters."

"Who from?"

Boston thought a moment. "I'm not sure. She got the call on her cell. I assumed it was from Beaton."

Gabby leaned toward Boston. "Nobody gives complete access to all the damn secrets in this place, Jonson. It just don't happen."

"It just did."

Gabby looked thoughtful for a moment and hacked a few times. "I was close to Barto, you know. I'd sometimes go up to his quarters an' we'd talk about things. Nothin' but talkin'." Her briar eyes sparkled and she smiled. "I've been with him and Toole since the early days and I think he almost

183

saw me as some kinda mother figure. But the way things went with him in the weeks before he died...there was somethin' big an' bad goin' on. It was like he was keepin' a close eye on even his own shadow-goin' around making happy and all, and then spendin' his nights just sittin' in that bare room of his with all them spooky statues, just sittin' there lookin' out the window into the fog, mutterin' about how everybody was out to get him an' things goin'on behind his back. Seemed real strange for a man as strong as him to be endin' like that. Toward the end, he didn't even trust me. Told me to get the hell out the last time I was up, 'bout two weeks ago."

"Did he say who was doing things behind his back?"

"Naw. Just the same old same old-They."

"It was Beth who mentioned the top secret project, just before she died. She said that it had to have been something big, and so secret that even the people in IT were kept in the dark about exactly what was going on. Could that project have been what had him spooked?"

"Hard ta say. Coulda bin, though."

"The management hierarchy here just seems so tight. There doesn't seem to be many people who have control. Seems it would be impossible to keep anything really big a secret for more than a few hours."

"Not if they outsourced the damn thing, along with its management. Kinda thing goes on a lot 'round here. Helps cut costs an' it might even be more secure, you know, since the leak. That came from inside." After a minute of hacking, she said, "So your ballin' the walkin' disaster. Brave man." Another fit of hacking. "Got a little surprise for ya, Jonson." She pointed to the wall where Bethany had disappeared. It was open and Marlee was walking into the lab. Boston felt a tug at his irises.

Chapter 55 - Coffee For Three

She was carrying a tray full of coffee cups, heading straight toward them. Gabby stood up and moved away from Boston as Marlee said, "I thought you two might need something to spark up the morning."

"Even brought one for yourself," said Boston.

"Mix," said Marlee as she reached him and held the tray with one hand as she reached for a coffee with her right. It was at this moment that Boston noticed Gabby had moved well out of the zone of Marlee's influence and a flash of dread shot through his chest. He suddenly moved back and lost his balance on the nano chair, which tumbled backward as his foot involuntarily shot up and kicked the tray out of Marlee's hand and into the air. The cups held the coffee well as they flew up, but on the flight down, directly over Boston, they tilted and poured.

Gabby nodded as if in agreement that the universe was unfolding predictably. Marlee looked on with the air of one resigned to one's fate. Boston stared up in horror as the steaming coffee descended toward him. About the same time the coffee splashed onto his blue Maui hula hula shirt, Marlee had her hand inside her robe and was taking out her flask of rubbing alcohol. By the time the hot liquid had penetrated Boston's shirt and begun to sear painfully across his chest, Marlee had taken a sizable swig from the flask and was passing it to Gabby, who took a swig just as Boston screamed.

He jumped up, wiping futilely at his shirt. Gabby pulled a first aid kit out of a drawer in a lab desk and opened it. She rummaged as Boston held the shirt out from his skin. Steam curled around his collar. Marlee took another swig from her flask. Gabby walked over to Boston, whose face was bright red, and told him to unbutton his shirt. He practically tore the buttons off. Gabby squeezed something from a tube and rubbed it onto Boston's crimson chest.

The red and the pain drained from his face immediately. He took a deep breath, touched his chest, which was back to its normal color-orange, from the orange chest hair.

"What is that stuff?" he said.

"Something one of our people put together in his spare time," said Gabby.

"You should be selling the stuff."

"Anything that comes outta this buildin' is the property of this damn buildin'. Not much incentive except to save some pain in the labs. People here got weird hobbies."

"Sorry," said Marlee. She was stooped over, picking up the tray and the empty cups. "It's like I said, I'm a klutz. It spreads into the people around me and draws the disaster right out of..."

"That was my fault," said Boston. "You were trying to do something nice and I freaked for no reason."

"OK."

"OK?"

"OK...it was your fault. Have a drink with me?" She held the flask out to him.

"Maybe when this is all over."

Marlee passed the flask to Gabby, who knocked back a stiff one. "Does everybody around here drink that stuff?" asked Boston.

"Yes," said Gabby and Marlee in unison.

"'cept maybe a few corporate jockeys-that Moore woman an' a few others," said Gabby. "Those ones 're already off their rockers. Keeps the rest of us from goin' just as nuts." She passed the flask back to Marlee who twisted the cap on and put it back under her robe.

"So you can get us back into the catacombs?" she said.

"Easy as pie," said Gabby. "Maybe too easy."

"Too easy?" said Boston.

"Got you both top level access to every room, hall, elevator and secret stairway in the buildin'," she said. "No access denied flags, nothin', just total access. Even I can't get you that kinda access, but I just did, and your beau just got carte blanche information access. Things're brewin' to a head an' I ain't stickin' around fer when the shit hits the fan." She pointed to a dark corner a few feet away from the elevator where two bulging suitcases leaned against the wall.

"You're leaving?" said Marlee.

"Like I said, shit's gonna hit the fan, girl," said Gabby. "Your man here's stirrin' it up good 'an it's gonna be messy. I'm outta here to someplace with no fog. I hate fog."

"But your contract…"

"Contract be damned. This place is goin' down. Might wanna get out yourself soon's possible."

188

"One more little thing though," said Boston.

"What's that, gorgeous?"

"You said that it was strange the amount of access you could get us. Where would that come from?"

"These days-could be anywhere." She winked and coughed and hacked and walked to the wall, picked up her suitcases and disappeared into the elevator.

Chapter 56 - Emergency Ration Packs

"Lost your bodyguard again, hon?" said Marlee after the elevator door closed on Gabby.

"Took off without a word. Guess there's more important things going on around here than me snooping and opening up sore points." He buttoned his shirt as he spoke. "That stuff works great. Too bad they don't have something to dry the shirt and remove the stains." He caught the pained look in Marlee's eyes and quickly added, "But I've got lots more shirts and this one will dry fast. And it was my fault."

"I told you…"

He twisted in the last button, took Marlee by her arms and planted a kiss on her pout. "You make things interesting."

"Isn't that a Chinese curse?"

"You're not Chinese." He kissed her on the nose. "By the way, did you hear about a bunch of prominent scientists arriving here a few months ago, about the same time as the project Beth was talking about started?"

"No, but that doesn't mean they didn't. Hundreds of people come in and out of this building every day. The main hall is like Grand Central Station seven days a week. Why?"

"Gabby mentioned it. Said she saw them here, and now some of them have disappeared."

"God knows what kind of contract they might have signed."

"You think Nobel laureates would sign a contract requiring them to just disappear for who knows how long without even their friends and families knowing what's going on?"

"Look around you."

Boston looked around at the ancient looking walls, rib-vaulted ceiling, backlit arched stained glass windows and heavy wooden lab benches, their surfaces covered with some of the most sophisticated scientific apparatus in the world. "You've got a point," he said. "And I think Gabby's right about the shit hitting the fan soon. Things could get dangerous and I don't want you to get..."

"No way!" Marlee put a finger over Boston's lips. "You're not getting rid of me. I'm in this till the end. That's when I get you in my quarters and we get rubbed up together."

"Listen..."

"No! You listen. They know I'm with you on this. They can't not know. That means I'm already screwed. And when I'm screwed, I go all the way."

"That doesn't make any..."

"What's next on the agenda, sweetie?"

"You're not backing off on this, are you."

She stood, looking him straight in the eye, not saying a word.

"OK," said Boston. "But do I really have to drink that stuff when this is over?"

"Sure do. In fact..." She put her hand under the top of the lab table next to her and ran her hand along it as she walked slowly. She stopped and tugged at something, and pulled out a plastic bottle of rubbing alcohol, which she used to refill her flask. "Sort of like emergency ration packs," she said. "Where to now?"

"Apparently, I've been given complete access to everything in the building."

"My, my, aren't you the special one. So what are you going to do with all that power?"

"Talk to the person who gave it to me."

***

"But why?" he chocked. "I didn't tell anyone…" He coughed, looked down at the red stain on his robe. "You can't…" He closed his eyes and his head slumped forward.

The figure in the brown robe backed away silently, tucking something with the metallic shine of heaviness under the brown folds.

Chapter 57 - Thousands of Marlees Tugging His Irises

Boston liked the idea of thousands of Marlees filling the reflected horizons in the elevator mirrors. The tug on his irises was like the takeoff of a shuttle on its way to Moon One, but he had to stay focused and alert. A dangerous situation was about to become even deadlier.

"But you said that Mac Beaton hated your guts," said Marlee.

"That's what I thought," said Boston. "It's the effect I usually have on people like him. I kind of pride myself on that. In fact, if somebody like Mac Beaton has it in for me, then I figure I must be doing something right."

"So why would he give you blanket access to the Barto Burger Empire? As far as I know, only two people on earth had that kind of access-Barto and Toole. And now Beaton, since Barto's death."

"The last time I saw him-right after Beth's death-he had a strange look. I thought it was worry or something like that. But now, now, I think I may have been wrong. I think it was fear. I think Mac Beaton is afraid of something. Maybe he thinks he's next on the killer's list. And I think he's afraid that if he says anything the killer will move on him."

"But why not just go to one of the other offices and let the police, or you, catch the killer while he's safe somewhere else?"

"Worst thing he could do if there's a management war going on. He needs to stay here and stay on top of things, or he could find himself out of a job."

"But is his job worth his life?"

"Maybe he's playing dumb, letting the killer think that he's trying everything he can to get me out of here."

"But he hasn't really been trying to get rid of you. You said that he could have you out of here any time he wants, but he hasn't done it."

"Exactly. He wants me on this referral. He wants me to find the killer."

"But why you?" Marlee put a hand on his shoulder and laughed. "Sorry, hon, I forgot. You're the best."

"Maybe not the best, but maybe the one most likely to shake things up in a weird place like this."

Marlee thought a moment "That's why he asked for you specifically."

"You got it. He acted pissed off at my, let's say unorthodox procedures…"

"Ooo…big words."

"He knew about my reputation for stirring up shit to get things done, which made me the best choice for this referral, but he had to act as though my way of doing things was bringing him close to taking me off the referral, and I think he was genuinely unhappy that I was taking so long."

"He wanted you to find the killer fast so that he would be safe."

"You're right on today. Maybe rubby's not so bad for the brain after all."

"Hey, never criticize a girl's choice of beverage."

Boston laughed as the elevator opened on Beaton's floor. They walked down the hall to his office and went into the waiting room where the body of Beaton's secretary lay on the floor, face down, a pool of blood spreading out from the hood. Marlee rushed to the secretary as Boston threw open the door to Beaton's office and ran in. Mac Beaton lay propped up on the floor, his back against the wall, blood staining the front of his white robe. His mouth moved, working slowly around words that didn't come out. His eyes were wide with horror.

Chapter 58 - A Bug In the Drug

Marlee rushed in and shrieked, "She's dead!" She saw Beaton. "Oh my God! Is he alive?"

Leaning over Beaton, Boston opened his robe with his wallet's laser knife while he told Laurel to send an ambulance. "What kind of wound is it?" said the tiny image on the screen. Boston pulled the blood-stained robe away from Beaton's body and said, "Looks like a bullet wound."

"People still use those things?"

"Just send an ambulance."

"Coming up." The screen went blank. Marlee said, "Is there anything I can do to help?" Boston bunched up a section of Beaton's robe and pushed down hard over a small hole spurting blood from his chest. "Hold this down tight on the wound," he said to Marlee.

Marlee pressed down on the wad of cloth with both hands. "What happened?" she said.

"Somebody shot him." Beaton was still twisting his mouth. Finally, a word come out. "Jonson," he said, barely perceptible. Boston put his head close to Beaton's, turned slightly so that his ear was close to Beaton's mouth. "Who did this to you?" he said.

"I don't know. He was wearing…a dark brown robe and a…hood."

"You didn't see his face?"

"He was…quite well-hooded. And he had a large gun with a silencer."

"Did you see his hands?"

"I was, of course, looking at the gun. Not the hand." And to Boston's amazement, it looked as though Beaton's round fish mouth curled at the corners into a smile. "I'm not quite the asshole...you think I am. I requested you...for this referral because...of your reputation for not following the rules."

"How long have you known you were in danger?"

"For the last few...weeks. I came across a project...in the lower levels...not authorized." He coughed and a line of blood dripped from the side of his mouth.

"Does it have anything to do with the sarcophagi in the catacombs?" said Boston.

Beaton smiled and coughed more blood. "That was abandoned...one of the reasons Barto got Toole on board. Wanted to clone...entire head office staff. Control them forever. Clone himself...if he could. But too much flack over Rogers. Big PR fiasco."

"And that's why you were in danger?" said Boston.

"No...same reason Barto in danger. Other project. Kemper knew about it...worked on it...till he realized what was going on. Killed him. Said he would go public. Killed him."

"Who killed him?" said Boston.

"Same who shot me," said Beaton. "Kemper told me before...they got him. Said secret project. Told Toole. Said we had to stop him. Toole said no. Let him go. Nobody would believe him."

"Believe him about what?" said Boston.

"The Praeder experiments. Bug in the formula. Got out of hand. One of the scientists…got the stuff in his system. Ate himself to death…right in front of us."

"What do you mean…ate himself to death?" said Marlee. "That's impossible."

"Nano-enhanced Praeder-Willi. Started eating burgers. Supposed to make him want one a day later. He couldn't stop eating. By time we realized…his stomach bloating and still eating. He died. Wasn't supposed to happen. Just supposed to make a delayed craving."

"So you scrapped the project?" said Boston.

"Officially," said Beaton. "But we kept on trying to find a way…to control it. Then…Rogers got some on his fingernails. Ate his arm off. We closed it down. Sent everybody off to all parts of the world. But somebody set up…another project. Somewhere in the catacombs. Don't know where. Quite…unauthorized. Barto found out. Came to me with it. Accused me. I didn't do it. He…got paranoid. Not trust anybody. Even though he acted happy. Accusing everybody." More blood dripped from his lips.

"OK," said Boston. "You'd better just take it easy. Help will be here soon."

Beaton grabbed Boston's arm with a hand the size of a bear paw. His grip was like steel. "Listen," he said. "Don't know who…behind this. Killing everybody at top. Toole…probably next. Get to him. The project Kemper found…horrifying. Got to…stop them." His eyes bulged and his upper body arched. "Get to Toole…before they do!" And then

198

his body collapsed like a salmon soufflé gone bad. Air hissed from his mouth and for just an instant Boston thought he saw something. It wasn't a complete movement, more like the beginnings of a movement, with all the intent of the full movement. It looked as though, just before Mac Beaton died, he was about to wink at Boston Jonson.

Chapter 59 - The Red Moustache

"Oh my God," said Marlee. "Is he…?"

"I'm afraid so," said Boston as he pulled his head away from Beaton's. He took Marlee's hands away from the bunched up material on Beaton's chest and they stood. He hugged her and she wrapped her arms around his neck. He took her head in his hands. "I think it's time for you…"

"Forget it," she said, eyes flashing. "You're not shaking me."

"Then we'd better get out of here before the ambulance gets here. They know it was a gunshot would. This place is soon going to be thick with cops."

Marlee squeezed her arms around him hard, planted a mixture of lip and tongue on his mouth and pulled away from him. "So, we need to get to Toole before the bad guys and the cops. That the plan?

"That the plan," said Boston. "Any idea where we might find him?"

Marlee pulled a nanophone from out of her robe and pressed a button.

"Just how much storage room do you have in those robes?" said Boston.

"Enough," said Marlee, and then into the tiny screen in the phone, "Is Dr. Toole in The Crib today, Charlie?"

The screen displayed a thick red moustache and a patch of white skin surrounded by a light brown hood. The moustache bobbed up and down as the voice spoke, "Haven't seen him today, Marlee.

Might want to try his quarters. Doing anything tonight?"

"'Fraid I got plans," she said. She winked at Boston.

"So you *are* boning that CI guy," said the moustache.

"I believe that would be none of your business," said Marlee. "Can you let me know if Toole shows up, sweetie?"

"Sure thing, Mar." And the screen went blank.

"One of your boyfriends?" said Boston.

"Jealous?"

"Nope. Just wondering how many scars are hidden under his hood."

She poked him in the ribs. "Ouch! I take it back!" She moved in quickly, kissed him on the cheek and said, "Big baby. Let's go up to Toole's quarters, see if it's as wild as you described it."

"You won't be disappointed. Know of any short cuts to get there?"

Chapter 60 - A Killer Vibe

His breathing slowed and the rhythm of his body became the gentle rhythm of waves washing over golden sand on a tropical beach.

"I've heard rumors about this elevator," said Marlee. "It has all the aura of a myth. Some people believed it existed, but I think most just chalked it up to too much rubbing alcohol."

He gave his right brain the day off and gave it permission to take its foot off the brakes on his life, that rich field of vibrations and interplay of frequencies that defined the world and everything that moved and stood around him.

Marlee reached out and touched the teak and ebony inlays on the mahogany paneling. "This is the real stuff," she said. "Not nanoplast or any other fake building material. And don't tell me..." Her eyes fixed on the frames holding the mirrors. "Solid gold frames." She touched one. "Yep. Solid gold frames. This place *is* a myth."

He visualized breathing through his *tan dien*, a mystic spot just above his stomach and just below is solar plexus. He breathed in pure chi energy, filled his body and soul, and massaged his vacationing mind with it.

"And do you feel that?" She put her hand on Boston's arm. "I mean, do you feel that." Her eyes seemed to focus on the air all around her. "No. You don't feel anything. Nothing. It's like we're not even moving. It's like this elevator is sitting here waiting for Dr. John's quarters to come down to us instead

202

of us going up to them. How much does it cost to freeze time and motion?"

He let all sense of motion, sound, smell, and thought drift away from his being, just let go of it all and let himself float directionless in the not-knowing of self. His purpose farted and dissolved. His meaning burped and dissipated. His mind became a vast repository of NOT. He had no idea where his fingers and feet were.

"The VIP elevator," said Marlee. "The VIP elevator." Her voice was filled with the dissipating awe a myth become reality. "And we're riding on it. Yep, riding on the VIP elevator. Up to see the Doctor." Around her the elevator glowed warmly as only as a twenty million dollar ten-by-ten foot moving room could.

Then it did an amazing thing.

And suddenly all the peace and stillness rushed in on Boston. A brown robe furled across the expanse of his awareness like a giant flag flapping in a wind storm and something flashed with terrifying brightness across vision of his third eye. He opened his eyes just as Marlee grabbed him by the arm.

"Did you feel that?" she said excitedly.

Boston shook his head, stunned from the vision.

"Did you feel it, hon?" she repeated. Then she looked up into his eyes and said, "Are you all right? You look really weird."

"It finally worked!" yelled Boston. "It worked!" Suddenly every muscle in his face was stretched into a smile the size of the world. " It worked!"

"Of course it worked," said Marlee. "They spent millions on this thing and that was one of the things that made it so expense-it goes sideways. That was what that small sense of movement was. We're really going sideways to Toole's place!"

Boston looked at her as though she were nuts. It took a moment to realize what she was talking about before he said, "I wasn't talking about the elevator. I was talking about the vibrations."

"The vibrations?"

"It's a long story. I finally picked up on them. They told me their story."

Now Marlee was looking at Boston as though he were nuts.

"No. I'm not crazy. I'll explain it later. But we have to be careful."

"Why's that, sweetie?"

"The killer was on this elevator. Just before us. Heading to Toole's quarters."

Chapter 61 - A Flash of Brown Robe

The elevator opened directly into Toole's quarters. Jimi Hendrix-still frozen in poster-time-ground his Stratocaster noiselessly through the deafening amplifiers of myth.

"Wow," said Marlee. "You could turn this place into a concert hall."

"That you could," said Boston, remembering Toole air-banding thousands of watts of Born To Be Wild.

But now, the room was empty.

"I don't think anybody's home," said Marlee. "Should we check the other rooms?"

"We have carte blanche." He winked. "Let's use it."

"Wow," said Marlee again, gazing around the room. "I've heard so much about this place, but I don't know of anybody-other than you and Bethany-who's ever been in here. And now we've got the place all to ourselves." She giggled and quaffed a stiff one from her flask. "Should we check out the bedroom?"

Boston frowned. "There was a murderer on the elevator just before us…"

"Yeah, and by the way, what's all that stuff about vibrations?"

"Marlee," said Boston as he put a finger over her lips. "We need to find Toole. He's in danger. Whoever killed Beaton is after Toole now and he was on that elevator just before us…"

"OK, C.I. Guy, honey bunch, Mr. Serious, let's find the killer."

Boston leaned down and kissed her lightly on the lips. "Thank you." His wallet buzzed. It was Laurel. "Where the hell are you, Boston? The police are really pissed. They found the bodies. They have a million questions. But you're not there. Where are you?"

Marlee shook her head. "I knew we should have…"

"Who's that?" said Laurel, trying again to bend her head around Boston's wallet.

"Nobody," said Boston.

Marlee punched him in the stomach. "Hey!"

"Boston," said Laurel. "The shit's hitting the fan…"

"I know," he said. "But I had to leave. I think Dr. Toole is in danger. We're trying to…"

"We're?" said Laurel. "Boston, who's with you? You're not bopping the staff again, are you?"

"*Again*?" said Marlee, brows raised. "So I'm just…"

"Ah ha!" said Laurel. "It's not Bethany Moore, is it? She's just supposed to be…"

"It's not Bethany," said Boston. "And what I do, and who I do it to on my time is…"

"Save it for the boss," said Laurel. "Where are you now?"

"In Toole's quarters."

"And let me guess-he's not there."

"We haven't checked the whole place, but, yes, I guessing he's not here."

"And you're not going to go back to Beaton's office and answer a million or two questions for the police."

"No time. Toole could be dead by the time they're finished, if he isn't already."

"I'll see what I can do to keep the police from pissing their pants, but you're gonna owe me big time for this one."

"You got it," said Boston and closed his wallet.

"So," said Marlee with feigned hurt, "I'm just another on-the-job roll in the sack, am I?"

Boston gathered her in his arms. "Laurel has some weird ideas about me. She likes to invent things."

"So you've never fucked 'the staff' on any of your referrals?"

"Well, I might have…"

"I don't want to hear it."

"Good. We need to search this place fast and…"

A movement near the elevator door caught Boston's attention. "Hey!" he yelled as a brown-robed figure rushed into the elevator and the wall closed over the opening. Boston and Marlee rushed toward the wall as it solidified over the elevator opening.

"That was the murderer!" said Boston. He turned quickly toward the room. "We need to search this place fast!"

They rushed through Toole's bedroom, washroom, a library with huge picture windows overlooking the fog, and a personal lab that was, surprisingly, unlocked and, even more surprisingly, unexceptional. "You'd think he'd have something ground-breaking that wouldn't be in the rest of the building," Marlee said with a look of disappointment.

"You'd think, wouldn't you?" said Boston thoughtfully.

"What's that look in your eyes? What are you thinking?"

"I'm thinking that you just hit the nail on the head," said Boston, looking around at the two tables with Petrie dishes, a laptop, and some books and papers. "This isn't Toole's personal lab. It's somewhere else."

"Somewhere...?" Marlee's face lit up. "The catacombs! He has a lab in the catacombs, doesn't he? And that's where the murderer is going!"

"Is there an express elevator to the catacombs?"

There was.

208

Chapter 62 - Bethany Bethany

"Careful," said Boston as they stepped out of the elevator and into the cavernous room with its rows of sarcophagi stretching into the underground distance. "He's here."

"Toole?"

"No. The murderer."

"Where's Toole."

"Here."

"That's what I said."

"Listen."

"But…"

Boston put his hand over her mouth. "Listen." Marlee's eyes flicked across the ceiling, the stone walls, and the hundreds of sarcophagi. Her eyes came to rest on a section of wall to their right. She reached up and pulled Boston's hand from her mouth. "What is that? It's like…"

"A voice. I think it's a voice."

"Sounded more like two voices," said Marlee.

"Let's check it out." Boston moved slowly toward where the sound had come from, head cocked to one side, listening. Marlee followed closely.

Around them, the catacombs were like a dark world at the center of the earth. Flames flicked and swooshed along the stone walls. The smell of ancient things filled their nostrils. "Oh shit," said Marlee. She grabbed Boston's arm and pointed at a brass name plate on a sarcophagus beside them. "Look," she said. "It has a date."

Boston took off his sunglasses and looked closely at the plate.

Bruce Wasson
2032 - 2068

"That would be the scientist who ate himself to death," said Boston. "From the first experiment." He looked at Marlee. Her eyes were wide. Her mouth was open. She was pointing at several of the sarcophagi around them. All their brass plates had dates. They all ended in 2069.

"I think we just found our missing scientists," said Boston.

"Oh, my god. You mean…?"

"When they got what they wanted from them, they killed them."

"Some of these people are Nobel laureates. They…"

"They knew too much." He raised his hand. "Listen."

It was like an excited murmur, a rising and falling motion of two sounds with one sound rising belligerently over the other and seeming almost to wrap around it, and then the other fighting back timidly only to be wrapped again. At least, this was how Boston wrapped his own mind around what he was hearing.

He whispered to Marlee. "I think you're right. It sounds like two voices. Coming from over there." He pointed toward a section of wall, stone blocks flickered under the light from a brass torch. A line of light the height of a door cut through the stone as though a giant sword had sliced the rock and now it was oozing slow light.

"A secret door," whispered Marlee.

"No," whispered Boston sarcastically. "Not in this place."

She punched him in the ribs. He choked back an ouch. They were beside the crack in the wall, but the stone blocks were too thick to see into the room beyond. Boston put his mouth up close to Marlee's ear. "We have to open this a bit more."

Marlee grabbed his arm and whispered, "It's Bethany. Listen."

He held his breath and listened. The voice sounded far off, but yes, it was Bethany Moore, but not the Bethany Moore in charge of herself and feeding off her image on every reflective object within a mile radius, not the voice of a woman who could stretch a cup of coffee to quench the thirst of the Galilee masses. This wasn't the voice of a woman who had earned the reputation of a corporate trollop and bitch extraordinaire. This was the voice of someone whipped and complaining. And then there was a deep raspy voice. It was scolding and deprecating, beating Bethany's voice down scornfully. There was something familiar about the voice, but he couldn't put his finger on it.

He put his finger on the stone door. It moved.

"Good hydraulics," whispered Marlee.

"I'll say," whispered Boston as he edged the stones a little more. They could hear the voices clearly now.

"But if you had just let me fuck him, I could have had him under my control" said Bethany. "…just like Gansheng."

211

The raspy voice struck back. "You never had him under your control. He used you!"

"No he didn't. He loved me. You…you drove him away from me."

Boston nudged the stones some more. Now they could just barely see inside. It was a small candle-lit room. The smell of sandalwood incense filled Boston's nostrils. Marlee's head pushed forward under his arm so that she could see as well. In a high-backed wooden chair beside a huge intricately carved confessional, Bethany Moore sat with disheveled hair and splotched makeup, tears rolling down her cheeks.

"I could have had everything he promised if you hadn't forced me into…"

Boston and Marlee gaped unbelieving as Bethany's face suddenly turned mean, baring her teeth as her mouth twisted into a snarl. Her voice was deep and raspy as she said, "Promises, you dumb little bitch. The old man was never going to put you in senior management."

Chapter 63 - Self-Betrayal

Boston pushed the door wide open and walked into the room. Marlee followed close behind. Bethany looked up casually at the pair and shook her head. "Oh, of course it's you," she said to Boston. "And you brought your little girlfriend." Her face twisted and the raspy voice growled, "I told you so!" Her face loosened and bounced between disappointment and anger. "Will you please shut up. I'm hurting here, in case you haven't noticed!"

"Oh, smarten up, you…"

"I said shut up…"

"Make me!"

"I hate you!"

"Everybody hates *you*."

She turned toward Boston. "You don't hate me, do you, Mr. Jonson?"

Boston was standing a few feet away from her. Marlee was right behind him. "No, Bethany," he said. "I don't hate you. Are you all right?"

"I was." Tears streamed down her cheeks. She pointed at the screen in the confessional. "Until *she* ruined everything."

"She?" said Boston.

Her face bunched up cruelly. "Don't blame it on me, you little fool. You're the one who put him up to it."

"I did not!"

"You fucked him into it, slut."

"Go to hell! You were the one who was fucking him." She turned to Boston. "She's a murderer."

"Am not!"

"May as well be. You made him do it." She turned again to Boston. "She said she had to do it, that she saw his diary and knew that he found out about the PWX project…"

"Don't tell him about that!"

"Oh, stuff it! It's all falling apart anyway!" She gave the confessional the finger. "After Rogers ate himself to death, the whole thing was flushed down the toilet. But we had an idea."

"Speak for yourself."

She scowled at the confessional. "The Praeder-Willi drug was supposed to just create a craving for whatever delivered it a day later. But it was so much more than that. It was mind control. Complete mind control. The kind of control that could make someone self-cannibalize. Think of the implications! The applications!"

"Oh, right, go ahead and tell them everything. Did you check to see if they've signed non-disclosures?"

"Oh, just shut up!" she yelled at the screen. And then to Boston, "We could modify it to control any kind of behavior."

"We?" said Boston.

"Now you've done it," said the raspy voice.

"Well I couldn't very well have done it on my own," said Bethany. "That kind of science is complicated, you know." She sighed loudly. "Besides, it's all over now. Kemper tipped him off.

That wasn't in his diary. He told me that himself. But he didn't know it was Kemper at the time. But I saw Kemper put the note under his door. He wanted to meet Gansheng in secret. Kemper found out about the international team."

Marlee almost startled Boston , speaking up from behind him. "And then you killed them all. Some of the greatest minds in the world."

"But we let them keep their names." The smile on Bethany's lips could have curled the blood in road kill. "We couldn't very well let them wander around telling people what they'd just created once they put two and two together and realized what it was, could we? No. That sort of thing isn't done. Don't you watch movies?"

"But how did you get them all here without anyone knowing? And where did you put them? Where did they work?"

Bethany, smiling evilly, smuggly, pointed to an open door beyond the confessional. It was dimly lighted but Boston could make out the silhouettes of lab equipment. It looked like a big room. "Modest compared to some of the labs in this building," said Bethany. "But it did the trick."

"But something this big, all those people," said Marlee. "And Kemper was the only one who noticed? How did you get it by Barto? Beaton? Even with outsourcing, this had to…how did you get it by Peters?"

Bethany waved her hand by her crotch. "Peters, like most men, is a pig. But then Kemper blew the whole thing by trying to tip off Gansheng. I wanted to fuck him, but…" She pointed at the screen. "She

215

wouldn't let me. Said Kemper had to go. But then I saw Gansheng's diary. He wrote about the note. He wrote about not trusting anybody. He wrote about me, how he was just using me and how he was never going to promote me to senior management. If I could just have gotten Kemper on our side and got him to meet with Gansheng and smooth things over, we wouldn't have had to kill so many people, and that counts for something, doesn't it?"

Her face contorted. "He was using you long before the note from Kemper, you little tramp!"

"Shut up! Shut up! Shut up!"

"So she made him kill Gansheng," said Bethany.

"Made who kill Gansheng?" said Boston.

"Made *me* kill Gansheng," said a voice behind them. Boston and Marlee turned their heads in unison. In the doorway, dressed in a dark brown robe, gun in hand, stood Dr. John Johnathan Toole.

"Darling," said the raspy voice.

216

Chapter 64 - Cat Fight

"You did it, man," said Toole. "You effin' did it. Solved the whole effin' thing without even making a referral. You're effin' good, man. But this does create a whole new set of problems, doesn't it?"

"Doesn't really have to," said Boston.

"What's that supposed to effin' mean?"

"You give yourself up. Bethany gives herself up. You both do a few thousand hours of community work, and everybody's happy."

"Or," said Toole, "I get rid of you and your girlfriend and Bethany and I use the nano-formula to take over the world. Then, we live happily ever after."

"I see," said Boston, "the old world domination thing. I thought that was Barto's game."

"He was taking advantage of Bethany, using her," said Toole. "He promised me I'd be up to my effin' ears in tits and ass, and it never happened. Then, when it did..." He gestured to Bethany with the gun. "...he made her start having sex with him."

"And I'm sure Bethany had nothing to do with that," said Marlee.

"Shut up, bitch," snarled the raspy voice.

"Nobody asked you," said Toole.

"What do you mean by that?" said Bethany, voice full of hurt.

"I meant her," said Toole.

"Me?" said Marlee. "But I was only telling the truth. How come you never knocked on my door?"

Toole raised his eyebrows and gave Marlee the once over. "I've heard that could be effin' dangerous."

"Johnny!" said Bethany.

Toole smiled and gestured with the gun. "She calls me Johnny. Nobody else calls me Johnny."

"Please don't point the gun at me," said Bethany.

"Sorry."

"With a cool pad like yours and all your money, you should have been up to your ears in tits and ass, with or without Barto's help," said Boston. "You didn't have to kill him."

"Yes, he did," said the voice. "Gansheng used me. He lied to me. He had to die. Besides, he was going to close down our project, stop us from taking over the world. So we used the nano-formula on him. It's perfect. The nanos do their work and then they just evaporate into the air. No clues. He used me."

"I think you've both been in this place too long," said Boston.

"I think it's time for you to leave," said Toole. He pointed the gun toward the door to the secret lab. "I want you both to stand by the door. Do the wrong thing, and I'll shoot *both* of you."

"Does that mean that if we do the right thing, you'll just shoot one of us?" said Marlee.

"If that's what you want to effin' believe, Miss Dunn, then yes…that's exactly what I effin' mean."

"I think he's going to shoot both of us in any case," said Boston.

"Then why should we go by the door," said Marlee.

"Good question," said Boston. He looked at Toole. "Any reason why we have to move toward the door before you shoot us?"

Toole thought for a moment and smiled. "It means we won't have as far to drag your dead and rotting bodies into the effin' lab."

"You're not going to put me in my sarcophagus?" said Marlee. "There *is* one out there for me, isn't there?"

Toole thought again. "Yes, Miss Dunn, there is. But wouldn't you rather rot away next to your CI boyfriend?"

"I'm assuming he has no intentions of letting *me* use one of the sarcophagi," said Boston.

"All that money, world domination, up to his ears in tits and Bethany, and he skimps on a burial plot," said Marlee, shaking her head.

"Make them move," said the voice.

"She's right," said Toole. "Move. Now. To the door."

Boston and Marlee began to shuffle backwards toward the lab door and, before Toole could say anything, Marlee had reached into her robe and pulled out her flask.

"Put that down!" yelled Toole.

"Go ahead and shoot me," said Marlee. "But if I'm going out now, it's not going to be without a big swig of the good stuff." She started to unscrew the cap as Bethany suddenly leapt up and said in her nasty voice, "We don't need to move anything! We'll just..." She reached into her robe and brought

219

out what looked like a pencil with erasers at both ends. "We'll nano them!"

Toole's eyes went wide. "Bethany! Put that down! That stuff is dangerous!"

"Damn right it is," said the raspy voice as she moved menacingly toward Boston and Marlee. "Pure nano-formula. Unprogrammed. Nobody knows what it'll do once it gets into a human, but when it's finished it'll just disappear."

"Put it away!" said Toole. "We don't need it."

"She wanted to fuck him," said the raspy voice.

"Who wanted to fuck him?" said Toole.

"Bethany," said the voice.

"But you're..." Marlee, finishing a long draw on the flask, passed it to Boston, too fast. A small stream of rubbing alcohol shot out in Bethany's direction just as she came within an arm's length with the nano container held in front of her. A few drops of alcohol hit one of the rubber ends of the container and it bubbled up and began spitting synthetic material that obviously didn't like rubbing alcohol. Within seconds, the entire stopper was gone and a black substance slipped out of the container. Boston and Marlee kept backing up. Bethany looked at the black slime curiously. "Drop it!" screamed Toole, but it was too late. The ooze scampered along the container with surprising speed and disappeared into Bethany's hand without leaving so much as a bump or a trace of discoloration to show that something very nasty had just entered her body.

She giggled.

It was a girlish giggle that matched her playful ponytail. She giggled again. "I tickles," she said. "It tickles all inside me."

Toole stared at her, eyes wide, mouth open, gun pointed at the floor. Boston closed his hand over Marlee's arm. Bethany's face suddenly twitched and the skin on her forehead bubbled for a few seconds and flattened to normal. "Now, look what you done," she said in her normal voice.

"It was that little jinx," said the raspy voice, pointing at Marlee. For just an instant, the tip of her finger bubbled. "Her and her rubbing alcohol. She'll be the downfall of us all."

Now the normal voice was starting to get pissed off. "Oh, stop the dramatics you manipulative bitch. She's nothing to him."

"I can't believe you still want to fuck him," said the voice.

"Why not? I've fucked everybody else!"

"Slut!"

Her right arm shot out to the side and her hand bunched into a white-knuckled fist. She punched herself in the side of the head. Her eyes crossed briefly as she screamed, "Don't call me a slut, bitch!"

"What's going on?" said Marlee.

"Cat fight," said Boston.

Her left hand wound up and she slapped herself with a loud whack and screamed, "We could have had the world, but you fucked it away!"

She bit viciously into her left hand as her right hand punched her mouth. She growled and snarled and bit repeatedly. Her face and hand were slick with blood. It splattered onto her robe and over the stone floor. She punched herself harder and faster as she gnawed voraciously on her hand. She pulled her hand away from her mouth and slapped herself again as her other arm punched her.

"Bitch!"

"Slut!"

Boston tightened his grip on Marlee and made a dive for the lab door, dragging her with him.

"Stop!" yelled Toole and pointed the gun at them too late. They were through the door and in the lab as the gun exploded and a bullet spattered into the far wall. They dove behind a row of lab tables and crawled hurriedly on all fours toward the back wall of the lab. Boston had his wallet in his hand.

Bethany jumped through the door, still slapping and punching herself. "Where do you think you're going? You can't leave! Not now! You haven't fucked her yet!" Suddenly, her eyes opened so wide that it looked like her eyeballs were popping out. She screamed and bit into her arm as she raked her face with her nails. She lifted her right foot and stomped down hard on her left foot. She slapped herself again and screamed, "That's no way to treat a lady!"

"Oh, sorry, you fucking little princess. I didn't realize..." Blood sprayed from her mouth as it caught a twisting right hook that crossed her eyes again. "Why you..." Another slap. She bit into her arm and shook her head, tearing into the blood-soaked robe. Her face was covered with blood. "I'll kill you for..." Another right hook. Another slap.

222

Toole was in the doorway now, looking furiously between Bethany and where he thought Boston and Marlee should be. "Bethany!" he yelled. "What's happening to you!"

"Go to hell, four eyes!" She scowled, eyes popping with fury and hatred. "I hate all of you!" She slapped herself again. And again.

Suddenly, her face went blank. Her body stiffened and then slumped forward. She stood with her head bent to the side, eyes glazed over, staring at nothing. Blood dripped from her lips and nose and over her chin and onto her robe and the floor.

"Bethany?" said Toole.

A chilling grin curled on her bloody lips.

"What's happening?" said Toole.

Her lips shook and moved slightly as though trying to wrap around words that wouldn't come out. She looked at Toole and whispered, "It tickles."

As Toole watched, horrified, Bethany lifted her hand to her mouth as though to take a sip of coffee from her empty hand, and her face and hand seemed to waver like hot air on a desert highway.

And she disappeared. Her robe crumpled onto the floor.

Toole stared at the robe. He looked up and around the lab, gun following his head as he searched for any sign of Boston and Marlee. Boston yelled, "The police are on their way down, Toole. Might be a good time to just call it a day."

Without a word, Toole turned and disappeared through the door.

Chapter 65 - Thwack!

"Thwack!" said a bullet as it tore a chunk of rock out of the door casing just as Boston and Marlee were about to leave the room. They threw themselves against the wall.

"Maybe we should give him a moment," said Marlee.

"We can't let him get away," said Boston.

"But there's nowhere for him to go. The police are here. We're in a patch of fog in the middle of nowhere. He has a gun."

Boston thought for a moment. The smell of cordite and overheated rock filled the air around them. The high rib-vaulted ceiling, stone walls, and long rows of sarcophagi in the next room seemed suddenly more deathlike and foreboding than when they were casually hunting for clues.

"We could go to my room and drink the good stuff and exchange genetic information till our eyes cross permanently," said Marlee as she pressed against him. "You said that you'd have a drink with me. Time to pay up, lover."

Boston bent over and kissed her on the forehead. "I know this is crazy…"

"…but you have to go after him," finished Marlee.

"If I let the police finish, then I'm not Boston Jonson."

"Well, at least I got my way."

"How's that?"

"We gave him a moment…while we talked."

Boston smiled and kissed her again. He rushed out the door just in time to see the massive brass and wood door leading into the secret stairway close with its inevitable creak.

"He's taking the stairs," called Boston. "You can come out here now."

Marlee finished a long draught from her flask and walked up to Boston. "That narrows it down to only a few places he can go," she said.

"How's that?"

"Gabby said that it only has five exit points. Here." She motioned her arm to take in the catacombs. "The senior exec quarters area where Toole, Beaton, Barto and a couple of others have their quarters, and a couple of higher than normal security labs." She thought for a moment and frowned.

"What?" said Boston.

"And, of course..." She let out a long sigh. "It just makes sense. I mean, why would he go anywhere else but the one place that nobody in their right mind wants to go?"

Boston reached out and put his hand on her cheek. She looked frightened now. "Wherever he's going, it can't be that bad."

"Oh yes it can," whispered Marlee. She took a deep breath. "He's going to the top of the building. Outside."

Chapter 66 - On The Stairs Again

Even though Boston had put his sunglasses in his shirt pocket, it was still difficult to see in the artificially eroded staircase winding around and around seemingly forever into the simulated stone and ancient wood inside the enigmatic guts of The Spit. He almost tripped on a simulated loose ledge of rock.

"That," he said angrily, "is just plain crazy."

"You're surprised?" said Marlee.

They heard a muffled curse ahead of them.

"I think Toole agrees with me," said Boston.

"Toole's as crazy as this place," said Marlee. "Why couldn't he have taken the damn elevator." She cocked her head to the side. "Oh yeah. I almost forgot-this is the only way to the top of the building. To the outside." She was beginning to pant. She was in front of Boston, who was trying to strike a safe balance between climbing the steps cautiously and appreciating the perfect curves just inches away from his head. "How long have we been climbing?" she asked.

"Days."

"Feels like it."

"Has anyone ever done this before?"

"Someone had to at one time or another-maybe the builders?"

"Did they live?" asked Boston.

"I think we passed their bones half an hour back."

"Now…that wouldn't surprise me."

He grabbed Marlee's arm and pulled her to a stop. "What?" she said.

"Listen."

They stood motionless, staring into each other's eyes. Marlee whispered, "I don't hear anything."

"Exactly," said Boston. "He's stopped climbing."

"Maybe he died."

Boston smiled. "It is never that easy. Either he's reached the top, or he's waiting to see if we're still following."

"So what do we do?"

"Wait a few minutes. See if he starts to move again."

"And in the meantime?" She pushed her face close to his and pressed her body against him. Her breath was quick and hot. Suddenly, her tongue was in his mouth. It stayed there for a long time, long enough to make his head swim and his pants bulge. If his heart was pounding from exertion before they stopped, it was now close to exploding from the things Marlee was doing in his mouth. He pulled his head back.

"He's moving again," he said.

"Damn," said Marlee. Her face was more flushed than normal and her eyes had a drowsily lusty look. Her flask appeared at her mouth as if by magic. She took a quick swig, looked around her, and said, "Always wondered what it would be like to make out in a place like this."

Boston laughed and said, "That would be just about any place in this building, wouldn't it?"

"Point for the CI guy." She put the flask back under her robe. "It can't be much farther now."

It wasn't.

Chapter 67 - Hold the Concert and the Bands Will Come

They stepped out into the fog-chilled night and the sound of thousands of cheering and raving rock fans slammed into their ears. Stretching before them under hundreds of angry gargoyles and ornate towers was a hundred foot wide stage. Blue, orange and yellow spotlights danced across its surface. The cheering came from hundreds of directional nano speakers mounted on poles and placed so that most of the sound would stay at the top of the building.

In the center of the stage, John Johnathan Toole, short, bald-headed, wearing round eyeglasses, faded blue jeans and a Doors t-shirt, bowed to Boston and Marlee. "This is where we'll do our first concert. Effin' cool, eh?"

Boston and Marlee gaped.

"Hard to believe, isn't it?" yelled Toole.

They nodded their heads. "You didn't have to kill all those people, Toole," said Boston. "Why did you do it?"

"Why?" he threw back. "He was going to shut me down, that's why!"

"Who was going to shut you down."

"Gansheng! He closed down the effin' human cloning project, man. We were going to recreate the entire effin' head office staff. The research I would have gotten..." He looked down at his right hand, which still held the gun. "Oh this," he said, and threw the gun over the side of the stage. "I don't need it anymore."

Boston stepped toward him. Toole pointed at him. "No!" He reached into his jeans pocket. Boston stepped backwards. Toole pulled out something flat and metallic. A remote control. He pressed a button and guitar music thundered across the stage and bounced off the minarets and buttresses and grumpy old gargoyles. It was the Doors' *Roadhouse Blues*. "Jim Morrison would have played here with me!" His eyes were wide and bulging behind his glasses. From another system of speakers, the audience roared. "He promised me tits and ass and a 60s rock band. Then, he helped himself to my girlfriend and took away my band!"

"She wasn't your girlfriend," yelled Marlee. "She was just using you!"

"Oh yeah. Effin' rub it in!" He lifted his arm over his head and bent down at the knees, his other hand holding the neck of an imaginary guitar. His arm came down upon the guitar and he screamed. He rolled across the stage, banging away at the invisible guitar, jumped up and pounded his fists onto an imaginary organ. He jumped through the organ and ran to the back of the stage and clobbered the hell out of invisible drums. "This was where I was gonna effin' play with the band!" he yelled. "I would have been the greatest rock drummer of all time! Bethany believed in me. She said I could do it. Then effin' Gansheng took it all away!" With one mighty downward swing of both arms, he stopped drumming. Bent over, face streaming with sweat and condensed fog, chest heaving, he stared directly at Boston and Marlee. *Roadhouse Blues* continued to blast through the speakers. "I really meant it when I said I would learn to play the drums." And then he was spinning and running and grinding out air guitar music and jumping and rolling across the stage. He stopped for a second and pulled something out of his pocket. His right hand exploded with red and blue light-a nano beacon. It's light would be seen for miles, even through the fog.

He started running and rolling again, his mouth moving out of time to the words. Nothing was synchronized. He slowed when the music picked up, rushed when it slowed. "Rock n' Roll for effin' ever!" he yelled as he rolled over the side of the stage and plummeted over seven hundred feet to the ground, nano beacon flashing red and blue into the pea soup night, arms and legs pounding out Rock n' Roll as he disappeared into the fog.

Boston and Marlee stared at the section of stage where Toole had gone over. They looked at each other. Marlee passed him the flask. He took a swig. It immediately turned his head into fire. He coughed and sputtered and breathed in deeply, his chest and stomach expanding under his blue Hawaiian hula-hula shirt. He let the air out slowly as a cloud seemed to cross over the inside of his head. "It does that at first," said Marlee.

He passed the flask back to her. He couldn't talk. "You get used to it."

Then he started to giggle. Marlee smiled. "What?"

He tried to speak a few times, but the alcohol was strangling his speech mechanism. He breathed deeply a few times and finally managed to get some words out. "Now…now we…now we know where the armies of ghosts came from."

They laughed and laughed. And then they went down to Marlee's quarters for another drink.

Chapter 68 - Burial Place

A strange and lonely quiet permeated the air around Gansheng Barto's chair. It was the kind of quiet that crept into the void left by death. Gansheng Barto would never again sit in the high-backed red leather chair and gaze through the huge windows into the roiling fog. The marble statues smirked and winked as usual, but the imagined life behind the stone eyes seemed robbed of force with Barto's passing.

Fog curled and twisted and danced up against the giant glass panes like a wall-sized lava lamp. The chandeliers dropped light onto the circular checkerboard floor through the asses of spider-like bronze lamps, but the light seemed wasted around the empty chair.

The enigmatic balcony, its mahogany railings layered with dust, surrounded the room with its secret, unreachable by doors or stairs. On its floor, just over the windows, two beautifully carved Chinese funeral urns sat at an angle to make them invisible to anyone standing in the room below. Carved into one of them were the words Li Tang and the other, Chow Tang.

Chapter 69 - Starting A New Life

As Gabby boarded the shuttle craft that would take her to her new home in the Caribbean, she could have sworn she'd seen a flash of light through the fog in the direction of The Spit. It was a place she wouldn't miss, a place she would never think about again as she strolled along beaches under palm trees and drank rum-packed tropical drinks under roofs of thatched palm fronds. She would never drink rubbing alcohol again. She wouldn't have to, not with her retirement nest egg-the two hundred million dollars she made off the sale of Barto Burger's cloning process.

Acknowledgements

As with all my novels, everyone in my life participated in one way or another. The vibrations we emanate leave life-long impression-good or bad. Fortunately, most of mine have been good. As for the bad ones, well, I uh, I kill their owners off in my stories. But then, there are those who've left wonderful vibrations, but I killed them off anyway. For instance, Beth Ashton. Beth is one of those very special people, one of those who make the rest of us sometimes wonder where we left our hearts. At a bus stop somewhere out by Zeeland? Under a bench at High Park? In the freezer? Beth never wonders about these things-she's too busy doing the things that show her heart to be well-rooted in her heart, working for the Run for the Cure, collecting hair for cancer patients (she got a good the top part of mine when John Jonathan Toole shaved it off-WhiteFeather got the pony tail for one of her spirit dolls), volunteering for dozens of other charities and worthy causes, and on top of all that, being there for her friends, unquestioningly and unconditionally. But I killed her off in this novel. Beth is Sara Beth, Marlee's friend. But I don't feel bad about killing her. She asked for it. In fact, she paid for it. You see, a few years ago, I ran an auction at eBay. The item? The right to be murdered off in Murder by Burger and get to choose the way you die. Beth, being a computer technician, chose a true computer geek way to check out-death by chocolate-coated coffee bean. But I just want you to understand this-Beth never did, does not, and never will drink rubbing alcohol. I did once, but that's another story.

I also killed John Heinstein. Sort of. I used John to model Dr. John Jonathan Toole. The characterization evolved. Well, no-it just plain changed. John is another computer geek. And a member-along with me and a bunch of other people-of the BlackTop MotorCycle Gang. We don't drive bikes. We just pull reading raids all around the city and force people to listen to the madness. BTW, John is the one who shaved my hair off live on Joe Blades radio show the night after New Years' Eve, whatever night that's called.

I'd also like to thank one of my oldest friends, Peter Maclean. I killed him too. As Gansheng Barto. But all I really used as a description of him from a wedding photo, sans the blood-drenched masticated food.

And I'd like to thank Brad Parks for his helpful comments about Murder by Burger before I sent it in to Deron at Double Dragon. "Hey, Brad! If you're reading this...that's your name on the first sarcophagus! But you're still alive!"

And I'd like to thank the Second Cup Coffee Shop at King's Place. I wrote the entire last two thirds of Burger there. And now I'm working on another Boston Jonson story. One in which people are murdered in coffee shops around the city. Maybe one of them will be in the Second Cup?

236